"What?" she ques⋯⋯⋯ **smiled. "Why are you looking at me like that?"**

"You're a beautiful woman."

Alana cleared her throat. "Thanks." She sat coyly with her eyes cast downward as she fiddled with the handle of her bag!

"Oh, now you're shy?" Drew teased.

"Whatever, Drew!" Alana pulled the door handle to get out.

Drew grabbed her arm to stop her. When she turned, he leaned toward her and kissed her lips. At first Alana didn't move, but Drew refused to let go. Pulling her closer, he kissed her again and continued kissing her until she kissed him back. Drew slid his hand behind her head and deepened the kiss. Her hand rested on his chest. When Drew finally released her, he had to catch his breath.

Alana sat back for a moment. Drew sat back as well, giving her a moment to collect herself. Alana licked her lips, which made Drew smile.

"I need to catch my train." Alana stepped out of the car.

"Have a good day." Drew's eyes followed her up the escalator and onto the platform before he took off. He was getting closer.

Dear Reader,

I hope you will enjoy getting to know the feisty Alana Tate and the handsome rebel Drew Barrington. Have fun taking this journey around the world as their love affair unfolds.

Alana has always been a hopeful romantic until her latest beau dumps her via text message. Now, she's losing hope about one day finding her prince. She makes up a list of rules to protect her heart. However, Drew Barrington has never been the kind of man that plays by the rules. Just when it seems he's successful in breaking down the barriers to her heart, an old flame returns to town. And she's got her eye on him along with a career opportunity of a lifetime.

Find out if the rebel player can be tamed, if the old flame can reignite Drew's fire or if Alana will finally get her prince. Enjoy the ride!

Ciao,

Nicki Night

RIDING INTO *Love*

NICKI NIGHT

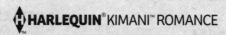

HARLEQUIN® KIMANI™ ROMANCE

Recycling programs
for this product may
not exist in your area.

ISBN-13: 978-0-373-86471-3

Riding into Love

Printed in U.S.A.

Nicki Night is an edgy hopeless romantic who enjoys creating stories of love and new possibilities. Nicki has a penchant for adventure and is currently working on penning her next romantic escapade. Nicki resides in the city dreams are made of, but occasionally travels to her treasured seaside hideaway to write in seclusion. She enjoys hearing from readers and can be contacted on Facebook, through her website at nickinight.com, or via email at NickiNightwrites@gmail.com.

Books by Nicki Night

Harlequin Kimani Romance

Her Chance at Love
His Love Lesson
Riding into Love

Visit the Author Profile page at Harlequin.com for more titles.

This book is dedicated to my Hero, Les Flagler.
Thank you for sharing me with my passion.

Acknowledgments

As always, I must start by giving honor to my Lord and Savior Jesus Christ for the gifts and blessings he has given to me. Now, for everyone else who has been an integral part of this amazing journey: my editorial team, Glenda Howard and Shannon Criss, thanks so much for investing in me. To my agent Sara Camili, I hope this "marriage" lasts forever! To my author-girlfriend, Zuri Day, and my fellow Harlequin Kimani Romance writing sisters and brothers, thank you for your acceptance. I love being a part of this amazing network. To Brenda Jackson, Beverly Jenkins, Donna Hill and Jacqueline Thomas, thank you for always being the wonderful women that you authentically are. I adore each of you. To my street team, thank you for helping me spread the word. To LaSheera Lee, thank you for your professionalism. You rock! To Les, my boo, my friend, my hubby and my biggest cheerleader, thank you for being fantastic. To my kids, Les, Milan and Laila, you are my inspiration. I hope I impress you. To my siblings, my gals, readers and book clubs nationwide, thanks a gazillion! Where would I be without your support? I dunno! Bryant Carrington, thank you so much for helping make this story authentic with all the super cool information about the world of motorcycles and racing. I sure hope I didn't leave anyone out. However, if I failed to mention your name, please know that I thank you and love you, and that you rock!

Ciao!

Chapter 1

Alana stormed into Payne, Tate and Associates, the law office she now shared with her best friend, Cadence, marched into her personal office and slammed the door behind her. Tossing her purse and laptop bag on the chair, she paced, her hands parked on her hips as she tried to control her heaving chest. She mumbled inaudibly before a light tap followed by Cadence's cautious entrance brought her out of her personal rage fest.

Cadence quietly walked in and closed the door behind her. "What's gotten you so uptight this morning? You blew through here like a tornado."

"I can't believe he did this!" Alana waved her cell phone in her hand before snatching her bags from the chair and placing them on the large cherrywood desk. She flopped into the chair.

"Who did what?" Cadence sat in one of the two chairs facing Alana's desk.

"James!" Alana sucked her teeth. "Can you believe that jerk broke up with me by text! By text!" she yelled. Her voice cracked. "Such a freaking coward! He said he can't do this anymore. He needs space. I smothered him too much."

"That's horrible." Cadence reached for Alana's hand.

Alana sighed. "Things have changed between us recently. I don't know what happened."

"Alana! You didn't tell me that." Cadence's hand went to her heart.

"I know. That's why we didn't show up last Sunday for the dinner you and Blake had to celebrate Hunter and Chey's engagement. He was supposed to show up at three. By six, he still hadn't returned my calls or responded to any of my texts. I was so pissed that I wanted to throw my phone but decided he wasn't worth the deductible I would have had to pay to get it replaced if it broke. I didn't hear from him until ten that night. I was furious." Alana's hands were balled into fists.

"Ten o'clock! Are you serious?" Cadence stood. Now she paced. "That—"

"Exactly!" Alana pounded her hand against the desk and stood too. "I said to him, 'Listen, Jackie,' which you know is my code word for *jackass*, and I lit into him so bad he was quiet for, like, a full minute before he spoke again. All his idiotic behind had to say was sorry. No viable explanation. Nothing! After being together for almost a year, I deserve more than just a weak apology."

Cadence's mouth opened, but she said nothing. She closed it again, shook her head and folded her arms across her chest. Alana raged on about all of the follow-up arguments they'd had for the remainder of the week.

"Did you respond to the text?"

"I left him a nice-nasty message. If he can't be man

enough to end our relationship face-to-face or at least pick up the phone, then he was never man enough for me anyway. He just needs to lose my number and my address and forget my name." Alana sat back down. She placed her elbows on her desk and rested her head in her hands. "I'm done. I don't even want to date anymore. I think I'll just put a band on my finger and tell any man who tries to hit on me that I'm married. I don't even want to be bothered."

"Oh no!" Cadence rounded Alana's desk and sat on it. She gripped Alana by the shoulders and looked into Alana's dejected eyes. "No matter what happened, you were always the one to remain hopeful. You always said your knight was out there waiting for you somewhere and you didn't mind rolling with a few frogs to find them because you knew he'd be worth it."

"I said that?" Alana chuckled.

"Yep. Always twisting up clichés to make your point, but I get it. I listened to you when you told me to keep living and practically pushed me on Blake." Cadence snickered. "And now, look, we're getting married."

"Well, I was wrong. I'm sick of these damn frogs. Screw that knight. If he is so worth it, then why do I have to swim through all this filthy pond water to find him?" Alana clucked her teeth. "He needs to come find me, shoot! I'm done, Cay," Alana said, calling her friend by the nickname she'd given her years ago.

"You can't be done. What if your prince is next?"

Alana craned her neck and looked at Cadence incredulously. "What the hell did you do with my best friend? Surely you aren't Cadence with all this 'keep hope alive' talk."

"I'm serious, Alana. Don't shut down. I did the same thing and it wasn't fun. I buried myself in work to keep from being lonely, but the more time I spent alone, the more I thought about all that things that went wrong with Kenny and me. I'd gotten over him but didn't get over the feeling of failing in my relationship. That's why I avoided dating. When I listened to you and started dating Blake, it was as if I started living again—laughing again. Trust me. That's not what you want. As outgoing as you are, you'd go completely crazy."

Alana put her head down. Both were quiet for several moments. "I don't know. This hurts so much. I thought he was *the one*, Cadence. I can't go through this again anytime soon. I'd love to have what you've found in Blake, but I'm starting to believe that's not for everyone."

Cadence hugged Alana, pulled back and searched her eyes. "You want the truth?"

Alana looked forlorn. "Sure. Why not?" She sighed.

"You fall for men very hard and fast. You have so much to offer the right man, but you have to learn to ease into relationships. Otherwise you scare men off. Save it for the right one. He'll deserve it and he'll appreciate you."

Alana breathed deeply and blew out an exasperated breath. Cadence was right. She hated to think of the number of men who'd left for the same exact reason. "So I need to be a little more discerning with my heart, huh?" Feeling raw, she chuckled timidly.

Cadence tilted her head sideways and nodded.

"I'll think about it. I still believe I need to take a break."

"Fine! Take a short one," Cadence offered. "And then get back out there and keep on living just like you told me to do."

"If I do get back out there, I'm going to keep my feelings at bay. If this next frog doesn't deserve my love, I'm keeping it on lockdown. Also—" Alana held her finger up as if she'd just received an epiphany "—I won't give him any of the good fruit! Not unless he proves himself worthy. This way, great sex won't cloud my judgment. James was great in bed…" Alana closed her eyes and moaned.

"Uh…" Cadence interrupted Alana's apparent moment. "I'm still standing here!"

Alana blushed and laughed hard. Cadence joined her and they could hardly stop themselves.

"See what I mean? Good sex will warp the mind, girl." She chuckled some more. "And lastly, I need to steer clear of known players. I think I'm intrigued by the idea of snagging a player. James was a player at first, and I'm willing to bet that other women had something to do with the fact that he went missing without an explanation."

"Sounds like a plan."

"Yep, that's it! I'll take some time for me and get back into the game. No falling too hard too fast, no sex and no players. That should save me some heartbreak. No man will ever be able to say that I've smothered him again."

"Good! Now, how do you feel?"

"I still feel horrible." Alana frowned. "I'll get over him—eventually. We actually had fun together." Alana looked at the clock on her desk that was a gift from a client. "We've got work to do. These clients can't represent themselves."

"You're right." Cadence lifted herself from Alana's desk and headed for the door. Just as she was about to walk through, she turned back toward Alana. "Oh, are you going to be free this Saturday?"

"I guess." Alana shrugged.

"Great! Then you can come by. Blake told me this morning that Drew will be in town this weekend and he and Hunter are thinking about having a get-together for Drew's birthday. Shall I count you in?"

Alana forced a smile as Cadence departed but didn't answer. The last thing she needed after this unofficial breakup with James was to be in the same room as the most flirtatious Barrington ever. Drew was an international player. Alana had witnessed his techniques up close for years. She had even entertained his advances and dated him for a short stint, which didn't end well. They made better friends. Admittedly, she enjoyed his flirting, but it was time for a change. Alana was done kissing frogs—especially gorgeous ones who were allergic to commitment and so skilled in bed that they could render her deaf and dumb.

Alana was also tired of heartbreak. Right there in her office, she made a personal vow to be more protective of her own heart. She wasn't breaking her rules for any man—especially not Drew Barrington.

Chapter 2

"Hey, Ma!" Drew yelled as he strolled through the first floor of his parents' spacious home on Long Island's Gold Coast. "Ma, I'm home! Pop, where are you?"

"Drew, is that you?" Joyce came down the stairs as fast as her middle-aged legs could carry her. "Happy birthday, baby boy!"

"Thanks, Ma!" Drew wrapped his arms around his mother, lifted her off her feet and swung her around. He planted a big kiss on her forehead. "Where's Pop?"

"I'm right here, boy!" Floyd carefully made his way down the winding staircase, taking one cautious step at a time.

"What happened to you, Pop?"

"Pulled another muscle at the gym trying to keep up with the young boys," Joyce said.

When Floyd reached the landing, he gave Drew a bright smile and shook his hand and then pulled him in for a hug. "Happy birthday, son! Are you staying for a while this time?"

"A few weeks. I'm heading back to Europe in February to train for the first race of the season in March."

"Oh, good. I can see more of my baby. I wish I knew you were coming. I would have had something here for you. I sent you a card. Did you get it?"

Drew nodded as Joyce headed toward the kitchen.

"Let's have a nice breakfast. I just bought some sage sausages. I know how much you love them," she said.

"Oh yes!" Floyd clapped his hands together and rubbed them greedily.

"Just one for you, Floyd," she warned, pointing her finger at him. "You need to watch that blood pressure of yours. It's been running high lately." She directed her last sentence to Drew.

"How are you feeling, Dad?"

Floyd waved away their concern. "I'm just fine. I could still lay you out if I needed to." Floyd put up his fists, bobbed and then weaved.

Drew looked at his mother with his brows raised and laughed. "Don't worry, old man. I won't put you to the test."

"Stop teasing your father, boy. Let him think he's still got it." She winked at Floyd. "Well, actually he does," she said, sauntering toward the counter.

Drew scrunched his nose. "That's too much information." They all laughed. "Ma—" Drew walked over to where his mother stood and placed his hand on her shoulder "—you always cook for me when I come. This time, I'd like to treat you and Dad to breakfast. Let's go. I'll drive."

"No!" Floyd and Joyce said at the same time.

"I'll drive," Floyd offered.

"Yes. Let's take your dad's truck. My heart would be in my throat by the time we got to the restaurant if you drove. I wouldn't be able to swallow my food." Joyce went toward the foyer. Floyd was on her heels.

Drew scrunched his face again. "I don't drive that fast." Both Joyce and Floyd stopped walking to look at Drew. "What?" Drew asked incredulously.

Joyce peered at him over the rim of her glasses. "We won't talk about that, sweetheart. Let's go have a nice breakfast. I'm glad you're here—in one piece!" The two of them snickered and Drew shook his head, chuckling at his parents.

He'd always had a penchant for speed, which is why he chose the life of a professional motorcycle racer over becoming an attorney.

The sanitation crew had plowed a narrow path down his parents' winding block, but once they made it to the main streets, the roads were clear. Within ten short minutes, they had reached one of his father's favorite restaurants for breakfast. Even at the early hour, the place was packed. Once they were served, conversation continued to flow without interruption.

"I'm thinking about buying a place in Manhattan."

"Save your money and take the guesthouse. No one has used it in years."

"Thanks, Ma, but I prefer the city and I need my own space."

"Yeah?" Floyd said, taking in a forkful of pancakes. "What about your house in Brooklyn?"

"The dude I'm renting from wants to sell the place this year and even though I'm hardly there, he asked if I was interested in buying it. I'd rather buy in Manhattan. I plan to look at a few places while I'm here."

"Will you spend more time in the States?" Joyce asked.

"It's possible. I'm thinking about making some changes in the next few years."

Floyd put his fork down. "You're going to quit racing?"

"No." Drew reared his head back. "Not yet. You know I just signed a new two-year contract with the Delgado team. I've been wondering what life after racing would look like for me. I want to begin preparing for that transition. There are a lot of options."

Floyd nodded and picked up his fork. "I can understand that, and I'm glad to see that you're thinking more about your future."

"I was hoping you were quitting. It's so dangerous. I worry about you so much. I can't even watch those races on TV," Joyce said. "Every time I hear about a crash, I cringe."

Drew smiled and placed his hand over his mother's hand. "There's nothing to worry about, Ma. Don't forget, I learned from the best." He looked at his father and smiled.

"I'm always going to worry about you. You and your brothers with your adventurous spirits have given me fits over the years."

"We get it from Dad!"

Floyd shrugged, unable to deny Drew's statement. They got their proclivity for adventure from him, a biker himself.

"Have you thought about settling down? All this traipsing across the globe and high-speed races don't leave much hope for grandkids. You don't want to be old and lonely, do you? Both Hunter and Blake have managed to find nice girls."

"I may get old, but I don't think I'll ever have to worry about being lonely." Drew rubbed his chin. His father laughed, but his mother shot a narrow-eyed glare his way. "I'm just kidding, Ma. I'll settle down one day—just not today."

Drew paid the tab, but they stayed and talked for a while longer. They left the restaurant and he spent a few more hours with them before heading back to his place to change for a night out with his brothers. They were meeting at Blake's condominium. As he dressed, he responded to various calls and texts from friends, mostly women wishing him a happy birthday. A few even offered to help him celebrate. One sent him a message with a picture of her lying across the bed with the words *Happy Birthday* written across her bare breasts. That gave Drew a laugh as he reminisced about the week he'd spent with her in Valencia, Spain, during the fall. The daughter of a Spanish dignitary, Lucia loved adventure as much as he did. She always made time to see him when his work brought him to her homeland, but his casual rendezvous with her was over.

Donned in all black with a fresh haircut and a sparkling diamond in his ear, Drew headed for Blake's place. During the ride, he actually thought about calling Lucia. It wouldn't take much for her to hop a plane and meet him for a birthday rendezvous. However, he had already planned to take care of a lot of business during his stay in New York and she would certainly be a huge distraction. He silently applauded himself for always being one to know his priorities. Occupied with all the thinking he'd done about his women and his plans, Drew made it to Blake's in no time. One thing he did decide was that it was definitely time for some changes.

The snow crunched under Drew's tires as he drove into an available space. He pulled his coat together at the collar, hopped out the car and ran to Blake's door. Drew heard music and several voices and assumed his cousins were partying with them. Eager to get the night started, he rang the bell several times to pierce the chatter.

Blake swung the door open and, before Drew could say a word, the crowd behind Blake yelled, "Surprise!"

"Oh!" Drew's hand covered his gaping mouth as he reared back. He bent over laughing. Hunter hugged Drew and then Blake pulled him in for a hug. Drew made his way through the crowd, greeting his guests. "Wait!" Everyone stopped and set their focus on Drew. "Does this mean we're not going out?"

Blake swatted him on the head. "The party is here, fool."

Drew sauntered over to the bar and grabbed a bottle of cognac and held it in the air. "Then let's get this party started!"

The guests cheered. Hunter cranked up the music and Drew started dancing right where he stood. Cadence went up to Drew, danced with him for a moment and then hugged him, wishing him a happy birthday before heading back to dance with Blake. Still holding his bottle, Drew continued through the mass of folks, hugging, chatting and giving high fives.

Someone pulled his arm. Drew turned around to his ex Stacey, who attended prep school with the brothers before becoming a Wall Street executive and moving to the same complex as Blake.

"Stacey?" Drew said unbelievingly.

"Yep! I haven't seen you in years. You're looking good." She nodded her approval.

"Thanks." She smiled wide as Drew looked her over from head to toe, pleased with how well her curves filled her little black dress. He lifted her arm and twirled her around. "You're looking pretty damn fine yourself, lady. What's up with you these days?"

"I'm well. I've watched some of your races."

Drew lifted his brows. "Really? That's cool."

They danced for a few songs as more guests arrived. When Hunter opened the door and Alana appeared in the doorway, Drew's focus shifted instantly. Alana arrived alone. He watched as she walked in and embraced Blake, Hunter and Chey before walking off with Cadence. He admired her silky-straight hair as it gracefully framed her face and flowed below her shoulders. He watched her hips sway under her electric-blue dress and allowed his eyes to roam over her legs concealed in black stockings to the sexy pair of high-heeled riding boots. He imagined how sweet she must have smelled, remembering what type of fragrances she preferred. Drew continued to watch as she and Cadence disappeared behind the wall separating the kitchen from the living room and wondered if she had noticed him. Suddenly, he wasn't so interested in Stacey's whereabouts in recent years. He didn't want to be rude, so he continued dancing and chatting with Stacey, but Alana had stolen his focus.

Chapter 3

Alana tried to act as if she hadn't noticed Drew, but who could miss that smooth, caramel skin; those dreamy, hooded eyes; broad shoulders; and slim waist wrapped in mysterious black. She had taken all of that in and more on her walk from the front door to the kitchen, including the fact that he was dancing with a pretty woman.

At first, Alana wasn't going to come, but Cadence kept calling to make sure she did. Besides, she had never been a homebody and was bored sitting at her place, alone. Her only sister, Adriana, lived in Chicago and her parents were busy socialites with plans of their own.

Alana grabbed the tray that Cadence had asked her to get and followed her through the crowd to the table with the food. Cadence made room for the additional trays and Alana put hers down. She turned and bumped right into Drew.

"Hey, Drew! Happy birthday!" she cheerfully yelled

over the symphony of voices, laughter and music. Alana gave him a friendly hug as if his sexy aura had no effect on her. Drew pulled her in tight and released her slowly. She tried not to swoon from the masculine scent of his cologne or the feeling of his taut chest against hers. Alana cleared her throat and stepped back, adding space between them.

"Thank you." He licked his lips and Alana wanted to touch them.

"Are you having a good time?" she asked.

"I'm having a great time now that you're here."

Alana twisted her lips. "You're such a flirt."

"I'm serious." He stared directly into her eyes. "You know we always had fun."

"That's true." Alana withdrew her hand from his, just realizing that he was holding on to it. "Well, enjoy yourself. I need to go back and finish helping Cadence."

"We'll talk later?"

Alana smiled and walked away.

After she had assisted Cadence refreshing the food and beverages, she got a drink and parked herself in a chair on the opposite side of the room from where Drew stood entertaining guests. It was obvious that he was being his usual self as those he was talking to were holding their stomachs, laughing. He always had wild tales for the guys. The song changed and the woman Drew had been dancing with when Alana first arrived ran over to him and dragged Drew to the dance floor. For the next three and a half minutes, she gyrated against him, flipped her hair and bent over, giving him a wide-ranging view of her backside. A crowd formed around them, cheering them on. Drew looked like he enjoyed every minute of it.

The song changed again. This time it was one of Alana's favorites. She stood and started dancing, singing along with the artist. Lost in her own musical euphoria, Alana swayed to the beat with her eyes closed. She felt a pair of hands on her waist and opened her eyes to find Drew dancing in front of her.

Drew leaned close to her ear. "Can I have this dance?" His low, husky tone sent shivers down her back.

Still dancing, Alana shrugged. Drew took her by the hand and led her to the center of the living room where Blake's coffee table usually sat. Together they danced song after song until both were glistening with sweat. His sexy moves taunted her, reminding her of the few intimate encounters they shared in the past. He was as skilled at dancing as he was at making love. The room felt warmer and that wasn't just because she was burning calories. Drew's presence caused enough heat to spark global warming.

"I really need a break," Alana panted, but when she tried to leave, Drew pulled her close to him and kept dancing. Laughing, she gave in and danced until the chemistry between them sizzled and threatened to catch fire, consuming the two of them in front of the entire room.

Alana finally peeled herself away from his magnetism, leaving him on the dance floor. She had to. Being so close to him was getting the best of her. In the short amount of time it took her to grab a bottle of water and chug half of it down, the woman whom Drew had been dancing with earlier had sidled back up to him. A sly grin played on her lips, but little did she know that Alana was grateful to be able to get away.

It was well into the night before the party began to thin out. Alana eventually found out the name of Drew's old friend, who remained by his side almost until the end. Alana, Blake, Cadence, Chey, Hunter, Drew, Stacey and a few others sat comfortably in the living room laughing and joking around. The ladies had removed their shoes and sat on the couch and the floor. Stacey sat so close to Drew that a toothpick wouldn't have fit between them. She stretched her lean frame over Drew during every exaggerated laugh, finding everything that he said funnier than anyone else in the room had. It was almost sickening. Alana wondered if anyone else had noticed, but she wouldn't dare make mention of it. Despite Stacey conspicuously throwing herself all over Drew, Alana continued to catch the penetrating stares he cast her way—so intense that she stopped looking in his direction all together.

Stacey could have Drew for all Alana cared. Entertaining him would challenge all of Alana's new rules and could only lead to the despair that she wanted to protect herself from. Still, she felt a twinge of jealousy.

Alana stood. "Cay, let me help you clean up before I head home."

"Oh yes. Thanks!" Cadence stood.

It wasn't Alana's intention, but that broke up the party. Everyone else got up to help clean. Blake turned up the music as they carried ravaged food trays and empty liquor bottles to the kitchen. Drew stood and Stacey followed his lead.

"Sit down, Drew. It's your birthday. You don't have to clean up."

"That's very nice of you, Cadence, but I wouldn't feel right sitting here watching everyone else work."

"I'll help too," Stacey said, and finally pitched in.

Drew grabbed a garbage bag and Stacey started filling it with cups and plates that people had left behind. Blake took down the decorations and Hunter and Chey folded up the tables.

Within a short time, the men were moving the furniture back into place, making Blake's condo look like his home again.

Alana headed to the coat closet. Drew was on her heels and Stacey was on his. Alana figured that would allow her a clean break. She needed to put as much distance between her and Drew as possible.

"Bye, guys!" Alana hugged everyone. "It was nice meeting you, Stacey."

"You too." Stacey's smile was unconvincing.

"Blake, don't forget we have a board meeting next week," Alana said, referring to The New York Association of Attorneys, a professional organization she, Hunter and Blake were members of.

"Oh yeah. I'll be there. I'm still trying to get your friend here to join." Blake pointed a thumb in Cadence's direction. She rolled her eyes at him.

"That won't happen! It's just not her thing," Alana teased. "Are you coming, Hunter?"

"I'll be there," he replied as he helped Chey into her coat.

"Great. Oh, Dr. Smell Good." Drew began playfully calling Chey that when he first tried one of her fragrant skin-care products. "Don't forget about my body scrub. I've already used up the last one you gave me. It was amazing."

Chey chuckled. "I'll send some with Hunter next week."

"Thanks, girl. That will be perfect. I'll send the money back with him."

"Good night, all. I'm pooped and I need to get these boots off. The balls of my feet feel like I've been walking on hot coals." Alana grimaced.

"That's from all that sexy dancing," Drew said, and winked.

Alana looked at Drew sideways and shook her head. Everyone laughed, except Stacey.

Blake and Cadence saw everyone to the door. Alana held her gloved hand over her pashmina to keep the frigid air from reaching her neck as she hastened to her car.

"Alana!" At first, Alana didn't hear Drew calling her. By the time she turned to respond, he was already approaching. "Hey, Drew. What's up?"

"I was going to walk you to your car."

"What about your friend?"

"Stacey? She's in her car." He dismissed any notion that there was anything deeper. "She lives nearby. She'll be fine."

"Oh. Okay. You don't have to walk me. I'm parked right across the street—see?" Alana pointed to her car. "It's cold out here."

"I know I don't have to. I want to."

That statement gave Alana pause. She swallowed hard but kept up her stride. "That's nice." Drew accompanied her across the street and waited for her to get in and start the car. Alana lowered the window. "Thanks again, Drew. You really didn't have to do this."

"Listen—" Drew said and Alana's stomach tightened. "Yeah?"

"I'm home for a few weeks. We should hang out."

"Sure. I'll tell Cadence to set something up. She's become quite the planner since she and Blake got together."

"I meant just you and me."

"Us…together…without anyone else around?"

"Just you—" Drew pointed to Alana "—and me." He pointed to himself.

Alana temporarily lost the ability to form a reasonable

thought. She couldn't say what was really on her mind, which was *hell no*! Buying a few moments, Alana took a deep breath.

"Listen, I know you just broke up with your dude."

Alana promised to get on Cadence's case for announcing her breakup to the world.

"I figured it would be good to hang out."

Alana hated that Drew was so charming. His eyes and those plump lips beckoned her. She remembered her rules.

"Sure," she said. "I'll talk to you later."

"Cool. Call me when you get home so I'll know that you arrived safely." Drew stepped back from her driver's window.

Alana smiled and, as she drove off, she noticed Stacey still sitting in her car, watching their interaction. She'd only said yes to Drew to avoid an awkward situation, but she had no intentions of going out with him. He was the main person she wanted to avoid. If fact, he had had his chance when they dated before. He hadn't taken it seriously. She'd had fun flirting with him over the past few years. Everyone assumed they would become an official item, but that never happened.

No sex and definitely no commitment-phobic players like Mr. Drew Barrington, she thought as she drove away. She already knew what Drew was like in bed and if any man had the ability to throw her off her game by way of incredible sex, Drew was certainly one of them. Also, Alana saw how Drew relished the attention Stacey lavished on him at the party and surmised that nothing had changed with him. "Good luck, Stacey. He's a slippery one," she said aloud. A player like him was hard to resist but could never be trusted.

Chapter 4

Drew reminisced about the way Alana had arrested his attention when she arrived at Blake's house the other night as he danced with Stacey. He remembered how her lips curled when she smiled, and those long sexy legs hidden beneath smooth stockings. Then, he envisioned Alana driving away at the end of the night. He had wanted to go with her for a nightcap. She intrigued and scared him at the same time, challenging his player status by causing him to desire her. Admittedly, he'd worked hard to avoid being caught up when they had dated before, because he couldn't imagine leaving her behind while he traipsed across the globe and he couldn't expect Alana, as dedicated as she was, to walk away from her profession.

Drew picked up his cell phone to call her and paused as his finger hovered over her name. Tossing the phone aside, Drew shook his head. What was he doing? Barrington men didn't chase women. Picking the phone back up, he called Hunter instead.

"What's up, Drew?" Hunter answered.

"Not much. Got any plans? I keep hearing about this new restaurant and lounge downtown on Atlantic. Let's go check it out. I'll have you home at a decent time so you can get your rest. I know you and Blake have a busy week coming up with this new case."

"That sounds good, but let me check with Chey first. I think she had something planned."

"Oh." Blake mentioning Chey made Drew think of Alana. He wondered what she was doing. "Hey, don't let me impose on your plans. You'll just have to take me there before I leave in a few weeks. It will be your treat for making me wait. Ha!"

"It's always my treat when I hang out with you."

"Well. You are the oldest."

"Yeah. Whatever, lil brother."

"Alright, Hunt. I'll catch up with you later. Tell Chey I said hello."

"Cool."

Drew put his phone aside and sat back in his black leather recliner. He looked around the four-story brownstone and noticed for the first time how barren that space felt. He'd purchased the home right after he had signed his first multimillion-dollar racing contract but only stayed there during the off-season. He spent most of the year at his homes in England and France, where he resided from March through November. Europe offered him a number of conveniences. Most of his races took place there. His time spent in the States was split between Brooklyn and his parents' sprawling home on the north shore of Long Island. He had inherited his proclivity to acquire interesting homes from his parents, who enjoyed dabbling in real estate as well.

Drew thought about calling Blake but figured he would also be spending this cold afternoon cozied up with his bride-to-be. Suddenly, he felt like the odd man out. He reached out to his cousin Lance, but the call went to voicemail. His other friends were scattered across the States and abroad, leaving him no more local options. The thought of calling Stacey came and went so fast it could have been a figment of his imagination. Drew looked at his phone, huffed and dialed Alana's number once again.

"Hello, Drew. How are you?"

"Well. Weren't you supposed to call me and let me know you got home safely?"

"That was two days ago."

"Well, you didn't call."

"You're too much. So what's up?"

"Nothing. Are you busy today?"

"I'm in for the afternoon. Why?"

"How about dinner?" he asked. Alana didn't respond right away. "Hello?" Drew looked at his phone to make sure that the call hadn't dropped and that she was still there. "Did you hear me?"

"Thanks for asking, but I don't think that would be a good idea."

It was Drew's turn to be silent. He couldn't think of any reason why going to dinner with him would be unwise. "Why not?" His confusion splayed across in his tone.

Alana sighed. "I just… It's not a good time."

"Since when has that made a difference?" Drew tried to keep his disappointment out of his voice.

Alana waited a beat before responding. "I'm sorry, Drew. I just can't go. I hope you understand."

"Sure," he said, even though he didn't.

"Take care, Drew." Alana hung up before he could answer.

"What the hell just happened?" Drew asked aloud.

Unaccustomed to rejection, he was puzzled by her snub. Women didn't turn him down. Even after their rendezvous, Alana had never refused to hang out with him. He tried to come up with a sensible explanation, but after tossing several scenarios across his mind, he still couldn't figure out why she'd brushed him off. Then he thought back to Friday night at the party. Had he done or said something to Alana to offend her? He couldn't recall and he hadn't been intoxicated enough to forget.

Drew got up from his recliner, grabbed his coat and the key to his newest SUV. Casually, he rode through residential streets of his coveted Clinton Hill neighborhood until he hit DeKalb. After driving a few blocks, he pulled up near the entrance of a crowded sports bar. Preferring not to be alone, Drew went inside, ordered a beer and settled right into the midst of the rambunctious crowd taking in the football game playing on several flat screens throughout the bar, which resembled a sports fanatic's recreational haven. NFL and college team paraphernalia covered the walls to the point where you could hardly see the wood panels. Sturdy tables stood erect in the center of the restaurant, flanked by green leather stools.

The Panthers rise to the playoffs had both excited and pissed off the hard-core New York fans that frequented the place. Collectively they weren't happy about the fact that neither their Jets nor the Giants made it to this point in the playoffs. The spectators cheered, cursed and joked about the plays being made. Drew joined in the fare, making fast friends. The camaraderie helped him forget about his earlier rejection. However, when the game was over and the chicken-wings-and-fries-eating crowd thinned out, it all came crashing back to him.

Drew wasn't quite ready to go home to all that quiet. Instead, he maneuvered down Atlantic Avenue to the Conduit, hit the Belt Parkway and found himself sitting in front of Alana's condominium in Long Island. Drew could tell she was surprised from the look on her face when she opened the door.

Drew stood before her, ignoring her perplexed expression while taking in the curves behind that tank top and sweatpants she wore. As casually as she was dressed, she still looked sexy enough to Drew to elicit a slight response from his groin area. Distancing himself from her allure, he refocused. He needed to understand what happened on the phone earlier.

Drew tilted his head to the side. "Did you actually say no to *me*?"

Chapter 5

A horn blew and Alana looked at her watch. Cadence and Blake were right on time. Ever since Cadence had told her about the evening's plans, Alana had been overcome with giddy merriment. She had stopped by her favorite boutique on the way home from the office to pick up the perfect outfit. Tilting left and then right, she now assessed her attire in her dressing-room mirror. Satisfied, she trotted down the steps in her spacious townhome, grabbed a full-length mink from the front closet and threw it across her arm as she headed out the door. She was so excited she barely felt the cold. It was as if her strapless jumpsuit were enough to shield her from the frigid air.

Alana could hardly believe she was on her way to a movie premiere and exclusive after-party. The lead was played by Christian Jacobs, her all-time-favorite actor, whom she thoroughly enjoyed fawning over. She knew he was married but wondered if his wife would allow her to give him a kiss if she got close enough. Alana laughed aloud at herself as she headed up the walk.

Alana whistled as the driver walked around and opened the door for her.

"We're traveling fancy tonight," she said as she ducked her head inside.

Her next words caught in her throat when her eyes landed on Drew reaching a hand in her direction to help her in. She hadn't thought to ask if Drew would be joining them when Cadence had invited her to the premiere. Nervous bursts of energy erupted in her stomach.

Alana cleared her throat and fixed a smile on her face. "Hey, Drew. How are you, Blake?" Her smile faded. "Cadence." She greeted her friend stiffly, upset that she hadn't given her prior notice—even a text—about Drew. Alana gave Cadence *the eye*, a look that was code for *we'll talk about this later*.

Cadence sunk into her shoulders just a little and smiled guiltily.

Drew. Alana took a breath and feigned another smile in his direction as the driver took off. Wasting no time, Drew slid over next to Alana.

"I know you received my many messages." He stressed the word *many*. She'd left all his calls and texts unanswered since the day he showed up at her door.

"I've been really busy." Though the interior of the car was already dim, Alana averted her eyes as she spoke.

"All lies!" Drew exclaimed.

Alana whipped her head in his direction. She couldn't believe he called her a liar—even if she did just tell a blatant untruth. Drew sported a wide Cheshire grin. Alana shook her head, glad that he was teasing.

"What's wrong? Do my good looks and charming personality make you uncomfortable?"

"Oh please!" She rolled her eyes. Both Blake and Cadence snickered.

"So why are you avoiding me?"

"I'm not avoiding you, Drew," she lied again. "I'm a busy girl." Another excuse. The night he showed up at her door, she'd told him that she wasn't feeling well in order to get him to leave. It worked. When he left, she'd laughed, tickled by how baffled he was at her refusal to go out with him. Drew was so unaccustomed to rejection that he couldn't comprehend the reality of that situation. He had still looked confused as he walked away that night.

"Okay. I'll accept that...this time."

Alana took a deep breath and turned to Blake. "Thanks so much for inviting me. This is so exciting. I don't think I've actually been in the midst of celebrities before."

Before Blake could respond, Drew jumped in. "You're welcome, but you've been around me thousands of times so what would be different about tonight?"

"Wait! This wasn't Blake's doing?"

Donning a proud smile, Drew shook his head. "I invited all of you. This is what I called you for, but you wouldn't answer."

"Well, then, thank you, Drew." Alana stopped there. She didn't want to make a big deal about her excitement now that she knew that this was Drew's doing. His ego was big enough without her efforts.

"Is anyone else joining us tonight?" Alana asked. She felt like she'd been duped into a double date. She noticed how unusually quiet Blake was. It was obvious that she was the last to know all the details about the evening's festivities and she was more than a little annoyed.

When the car pulled up in front of the theater on Broadway in the heart of the theater district, Alana was the first to get out. She didn't even wait for the driver to open the door. She stood to the side until all the others climbed out of the car and then hung back to walk behind them at a distance. Alana was determined not to look like she was on a date with Drew. But, gentleman that he was, Drew gestured for her to walk ahead of him. Taking quick steps, she was on Blake's heels, creating as much space as possible between her and Drew. Excited spectators stood behind stanchions, screaming and snapping pictures with everything from high-quality cameras to cell phones. Alana was too busy focusing on how far she was from Drew to enjoy the celebrity treatment. She assumed those onlookers would end up deleting their pictures of her once they realized they didn't know who she was.

Under the bright lights inside the theater's lobby, Alana noticed how ruggedly handsome Drew looked in his well-fitting tuxedo. She also noticed how women stole glances, smiled coyly or winked at him. He took it all in stride with the charm of a skilled player.

A stunning gentleman with sharp facial features and long, dusty blond hair spotted Drew, raced over and swallowed him up in a bear hug. Drew introduced the fellow as his friend and new Delgado team member. He was also the brother-in-law of one of the actors in the film, and the person who had invited Drew to the evening's festivities.

"Follow me," Sean said, leading them inside the theater. His French accent made it hard to understand what he said at first.

Drew and Sean chatted cheerfully as they walked down the aisle. Sean waved them into a row of seats near the front. Excitement bubbled inside of Alana as she recognized all the celebrities around her, mingling, talking and finding seats. She felt like a little girl on her first trip to Disney World. People whom she'd watched on big and little screens for years smiled, nodded and even waved as she made her way to their seats. She forgot about avoiding Drew until he plopped into the seat next to her.

The lights flickered, indicating that the movie was about to start. The cast entered the theater from the stage doors on either side of the screen. People cheered. Alana actually held her breath to keep from screaming when Christian Jacobs entered, made eye contact, smiled and nodded before being seated with his cast members along the front row. He had been within twenty feet of her. She wanted to fall into her chair but had too much poise to allow that to happen.

The lights went out. The screen lit up and music filled the theater. Alana put her hand to her chest and exhaled. This was certainly a night she'd never forget.

When the movie was over, they were ushered to their limos and taken to the private after-party at an enclosed rooftop venue overlooking Lexington Avenue. Alana was a born and bred New Yorker with a few well-established corporate connections, but she had never heard of or seen this place before. Alana looked around in awe at the all-white walls, furniture and carpet. As the place filled up, she wondered how the floor stayed clean. Several crystal chandeliers hung from the ceiling and sparkled in their reflection against the wall of windows that boasted a magnificent view of New York City's famous, glistening skyline. Servers in black bottoms, white shirts and white gloves passed champagne and canapés throughout the room.

Blake, Drew, Cadence and Alana found a comfortable spot to sit, eat the canapés and sip their champagne as they took in views of the skyline. They talked about how great the movie was and how lucky they were to have been able to see it before it hit theaters the next day. Music flowed and Alana was finally relaxed enough to really begin to enjoy herself. She still worked to keep her distance from Drew no matter how many times he parked himself by her side. She made sure her body language clearly told him to stand back.

Applause started as a low rumble and expanded until everyone in the room stood, clapped and cheered while the cast entered. Alana's breath caught for the umpteenth time that night as Christian and his stunning fellow cast members entered the room. All of them looked more exquisite in person than they had on the screen. Christian's wife was also stunning. Alana wanted to ask where she'd gotten her shoes and figured it was probably in another country. They went through the crowd slapping high fives, giving hugs and laughing as they greeted and thanked their guests and supporters, including Alana, Blake and Cadence.

Christian approached them and took Drew's hand. He pointed as recognition hit him. "You're Sean's buddy, right?"

"Yeah." Drew's smile was charming.

Christian pulled him in for a hug. "I saw you race last year in Qatar. A few of us came out to root for Sean."

"I remember."

"Good times!" Christian said. "You're on the same team now."

Sean walked up.

"Yep." Drew nodded.

"Now I don't have to worry about him beating me!" Sean said, laughing.

"We'll be at a few of your races this year. I look for-

ward to seeing you again and more partying, of course."
Christian raised his brows and smiled as if there was a
lot more to the idea of parties.

Surprisingly, Alana felt a slight pang of jealousy ball
in her stomach. She looked away.

"Let me introduce you to my people," Drew said.
"This is my brother Blake, his fiancée, Cadence, and
my...a good friend, Alana."

Alana didn't miss Drew's pause and wondered what
he meant to say.

They all smiled and shook Christians's hand. Immediately after Alana shook hands, she and Cadence headed
to the bathroom. Inside, she released the giggles that
she'd held inside so she could remain poised in front of
Christian and Drew.

"We shook Christian Jacob's hand," Cadence squealed.

"I can't believe it," Alana said. "I can't even believe
we are here with all these celebrities just chilling out
like regular folk."

Cadence refreshed her lipstick in front of the mirror.
Alana examined her makeup and decided that her lips
were in need of freshening as well. Cadence put her lipstick in her evening bag and stared at Alana.

"What?" Alana asked.

"Did you hear Drew pause when he was introducing
us to Christian? What was he about to say?"

"I don't know. I don't want to know and I don't care."

Cadence cast an unbelieving stare. "And I don't believe that."

"I don't have the time, tolerance or patience for Drew.
I told you. I'm done with players." Alana returned her attention to her lips, looked them over and put her lipstick
back in her purse. She turned to Cadence and raised her
brow. "And why didn't you tell me that he was coming?

Imagine my surprise when I realized he was the one responsible for tonight."

"They asked me not to say anything."

Alana narrowed her eyes at her even more.

"He just wanted to hang out with you and this was the perfect opportunity. You've been avoiding him the whole time he's been home and he can't seem to understand why."

That almost made Alana feel bad, but when she thought of protecting her heart, she refused to allow herself to be caught up in his web and brushed off that slight feeling of guilt. "You're my friend, Cadence. You should have said something."

"I'm sorry. They made me promise." Cadence pouted. "You forgive me?"

"Hell yeah! I'm having a good time!" Alana shooed her. "Now let's get back to this party."

Cadence paused just as they were about to walk out of the bathroom. Turning to Alana, she pointed. "Now that you know he really wanted you to be here, stop avoiding him. You've been doing it all night."

Like a scolded child, Alana tilted her head. "You have to be careful with men like Drew. I can't afford to let him charm me like a wild snake. Next thing you know, I'll be looking for my panties and wondering how my dress ended up in the chandelier. He's a wild one!"

Cadence looked at her for a moment before she burst with laughter. The ladies rejoined their party and had a blast meeting some of the celebrities they admired the most. Alana especially enjoyed the relaxed vibe.

"Are you enjoying yourself?" Drew handed her a flute of champagne. He was at her side once again.

"Yes. This entire night was incredible. Thanks," she said sincerely.

"I'm glad."

Giving him the lukewarm shoulder, Alana moved to the music but didn't continue the conversation. She assumed that Drew wasn't going to ask her to dance again since she kept declining his offer each time he asked. They stood on the sidelines watching Blake, Cadence and the rest of the partygoers cut the beautiful white rug. She smiled as she scanned the room, trying to burn this night into her memory. Who knew if she'd experience something like this ever again?

When her eyes swept across the room once again and landed on her ex James, who was staring right back at her, she almost choked. Where had he come from? She hadn't seen him all night. Who was he with? Not that she cared—anymore.

Taking Drew by the hand, she dragged him to the dance floor and pulled him close. Drew looked at her suspiciously but danced with her anyway. Cautiously, he placed his hand on her waist. Alana stepped closer, shifting his hands to her backside, and wrapped her arms around his neck. Drew's head reared back in shock and he smiled. She didn't. She was too busy watching James in her peripheral vision. Alana wanted him to know that she had moved on. Finally, James turned away, peeling his glare away from Alana and Drew, but then he planted a slow, soft kiss on the cheek of the woman next to him. She tittered. He looked back at Alana and grinned. She knew she shouldn't but leaned in anyway. When her lips connected with Drew's, her stomach tightened. Drew took that kiss as an invitation to go deeper and kissed her with so much hunger right there on the dance floor that he left her breathless. Alana felt as if she had been transported to another place. When they opened their eyes, Cadence and Blake were staring at them.

Chapter 6

Drew showed up at Alana's house early Saturday morning with a breakfast spread. He came for answers. She wasn't getting away this time. Drew rang the bell and knocked. When she finally opened the door, she scowled. Drew threw his head back and laughed.

"At least I bought breakfast," he said, holding up the bags in his hands.

Even in a robe, scarf and furry slippers she looked stunning to him.

Alana stepped aside and Drew entered her home. She led him to the kitchen.

"Thanks. Give me a moment to get dressed. I'll be right back." She darted out of the kitchen.

Drew had set up the table with bagels and flavored spreads from Panera Bread and Starbucks coffee.

After a while Alana entered the room, looking completely refreshed. Her hair hung along the side of her face to her shoulders. She wore jeans and a fitted T-shirt that said I Don't Sweat, I Sparkle. She still had on her furry slippers.

Alana removed utensils from the drawer and then plates and mugs from the cabinet and joined Drew at the table. It wasn't until she poured and sipped her coffee that she finally spoke.

"To what do I owe this unexpected visit?" Before he could answer, she started again. "By the way, you're going to have to stop doing that. I don't usually open the door for people when they show up without calling first."

"I have some questions for you." Drew studied her, trying to figure out what could be going on in that beautiful head of hers. "What happened? What changed?"

Alana huffed, dropping her shoulders. She took another sip of coffee. "Nothing happened."

"Oh, something happened." Drew stood. Suddenly he had too much energy coursing through him to sit still. "We used to hang when I came into town. Now you act as if you don't want to be bothered. You avoid my calls. I invite you out for an amazing evening and you ignore me half the night. Then, all of the sudden, you pull me to the dance floor and kiss me, but when we leave, you don't say another word to me. What the hell, Alana? What's all of this about?"

"What does it matter?" Alana stood and walked over to the sink. "It's not like we're dating or anything. Why do you care?"

Drew sat back down. She was right. He started to question himself for even coming over. Alana wasn't his girlfriend. She didn't owe him any explanations. Why did he care?

"I'm sorry. That was mean." Alana joined him at the table again. "I'm having a hard time trusting men right now. Whatever it was that you and I shared, it didn't end well. Besides that, I just broke up with someone so my wounds are somewhat fresh." She looked up toward the ceiling and breathed deeply. "I'll be completely honest— I thought things would have been different between you and me, but when your ex came back into the picture, you cast me aside." Alana shrugged and fingered the rim of her coffee cup pensively. "I acted as if it was no big deal…but that stung."

Silence ensued, allowing Drew to absorb the weight of her feelings. He hadn't realized how he'd affected Alana. He cared as much about her now as he did before, but he always assumed that their relationship had been a casual one. Drew knew then that if Alana was to ever trust her heart with him again, he needed to prove himself.

"When James came along," Alana continued, "I thought I'd found everything I was looking for. Our relationship started out great." She paused for a moment. "Then things changed… And now, a year later, he's gone. He actually broke up with me by text."

"What?" Drew's brows creased. "What kind of grown man breaks up with his woman by text? How old is this jackass?" Despite the hand that Drew had previously played in mincing Alana's heart, he was genuinely annoyed by James's juvenile act. Now he understood Alana's behavior a little better. He felt a need to lighten the atmosphere. "Were you robbing the cradle?"

Alana laughed. "It's pretty ridiculous, isn't it?"

"Yeah. Please don't tell me that was the guy at the premiere the other night."

Alana straightened up. "What guy?"

"You're such a bad liar. Now I know why you suddenly wanted to dance with me." Drew shook his head. "That's why you kissed me."

"Drew, I—"

Drew held his hand up. "Don't bother. I'm the master at this game and I don't miss much. I saw him way before you did."

"You did?"

"So you admit it? That was him."

Alana tucked her bottom lip into her mouth and looked down.

"He'd been watching you from the time he walked in with his chick. I know her. She's a talent scout. It seems you didn't notice him until the end of the night and that's when you pulled me into your little game. You wanted him to think you moved on."

Alana nodded.

"Don't get all shy on me now."

"Jeez, Drew!" Alana rolled her eyes. "You're right. Everything you said was right."

Drew laughed. Alana blew out a breath. They sat in silence for a while.

"Do you still care about him?"

Alana twisted her lips and stared pensively into space. "It doesn't matter anymore."

Drew looked at her in that intense way he'd become accustomed to doing, studying her as if he were trying to see inside of her. She turned away. Alana may have perceived it as scrutiny, but Drew found more to admire about her every time he set eyes on her.

"Is this why you're avoiding me?"

Alana's face became serious. She stood and began carrying the empty plates to the sink. Drew followed behind her. When she turned to go back to the table, she ran right into him.

"Answer me." He wasn't letting her get away again. "And tell the truth."

Alana closed her eyes and breathed in and out slowly. "I needed time. Dating wouldn't be good for me right now."

"I didn't ask you to be my woman. I asked you to dinner."

"I know, but…"

"But what? I don't understand."

"Drew! You're not good for me."

He reared back. "What's that supposed to mean?"

"Listen. I don't have any luck with relationships."

Drew opened his mouth and Alana held her hand up.

"Let me finish. Yes, I enjoy hanging out with you, but I don't want to subject myself again to what happened between us. I'm done with players and casual dating." Alana threw her hands up, punctuating her sentence to show how finished she was with those concepts. "I want more than that and I don't believe you're capable of more so I'd rather not waste our time. I really need to work on myself right now."

Drew held his hands up in surrender. "Okay. I can understand that."

He had other things to say as well, but didn't want to make promises that he wasn't sure he'd be able to keep. He'd heard the same story from many women before, but this was the first time that it felt like a blow to his gut. Alana didn't want to be bothered with him and he found that troubling. But what could he do when he was about to be on the road for the next nine months? He'd gotten the answers he'd come for, but despite that he wanted to kiss her again, like he had on that dance floor. He had suspected she was up to something, but he'd still sensed the hunger in her kiss and proudly left her with swollen lips.

Alana leaned against the counter and traced imaginary circles. "So now you know. It's not anything personal."

"That's cool." Drew watched her fingers, unable to take his eyes off her.

The atmosphere became tense and their conversation turned laborious.

"When is your first race?" Alana folded her arms in front of her but didn't look at him as she spoke.

"Beginning of March."

"Where?"

"Qatar."

"Oh. Wow."

"Yeah. I'll be heading there next week to get ready."

"How does a motorcycle racer prepare?"

Drew welcomed the change of subject but still wished he could somehow convince her that things were different with him now. "By working out and practicing certain skills."

"What kind of workout?"

"Well, arm, leg and core strength is important when it comes to handling the bikes, but bulk is not very good because it adds weight. There's a delicate balance. We schedule track days to practice. You should come to one of my races someday."

"But you don't race in the US, do you?"

"Sure we do. We have one at a track right outside of Austin in April. It would be cool if you came to a race overseas. That is, of course, if I'm not too horrible to hang with."

Alana pressed her lips together and swatted at him.

Drew laughed. "You'd like it. I'll get you your own hotel room so you don't have to worry about ending up in my bed having casual sex or something like that."

"Drew!" She swatted him again. This time she missed completely.

After a few beats of silence, Drew exhaled. "I better get going. I've got training to do today. I need to work off all the bagels I've been eating since I've been home.

Those are sure to slow me down on the track if I'm not careful."

Drew headed to the door, with Alana following behind. He reached for the knob, stopped and turned back toward Alana, studying her eyes again. She looked away. He continued watching her, willing her to look at him again. Finally she did. Their gaze connected and he felt the air swirling on the inside of his chest.

"Alana." His voice was lower, a little huskier than he intended.

"Yes, Drew?"

Her words felt like a soft feather against his ear.

"You think I'm not capable, but I am."

At first, Alana looked puzzled, but when Drew closed in on the space separating her from him, realization flashed in her eyes. Drew touched her hand. Heat passed through him, starting in his finger and settling in his core. He could tell by the slight shudder that she'd felt it too.

Before she could protest, he lifted her chin and softly placed his lips on hers. When she didn't resist, he kissed her again. She hadn't moved so he snaked his arm around her waist, pulled her closer and devoured her mouth. An intense hunger surged through him and he held her even closer. Drew kissed her as if she were a long-lost love whom he was in jeopardy of losing once again. Backing her up to the wall, he pressed himself against her. When he felt her hand splayed across his chest, he went even deeper, kissing her so passionately that his body began to respond. Heat pooled in his groin and he quickly released her, staring at her closed eyes and kiss-swollen lips.

Breathlessly, Drew said, "I'm coming back for you." He didn't know what compelled him to say that.

Drew needed to leave right away before he lost control. Tearing himself away from Alana, he walked out realizing that he was more affected by her than he ever cared to admit.

Chapter 7

Drew's kiss and sudden exit left Alana confused.

"I'm coming back for you?" she said aloud, repeating Drew's words and wondering what they were supposed to mean. Instinctively, she touched her lips and realized she was still breathing heavily. Drew's kiss made her feel weightless.

Alana shook her head, attempting to shake off the hold that Drew's kiss had on her. If Drew thought he was going to end up in her bed, he was mistaken. She was going to put a stop to him showing up at her house unannounced, as well. She didn't want to be rude, but she needed to get that message across to him.

She tried to convince herself that his advances weren't welcome and that his touch had no effect. Yet, he was stirring up a hunger in her that felt potentially explosive. His presence was a threat to her resolve.

Alana headed back to the kitchen to clean up the

plates from her and Drew's impromptu breakfast. She also thought about Cadence keeping Drew's invitation a secret and grabbed her cell phone.

"Pick up the phone, lady." Alana tapped her nails against the countertop as she counted the rings. Just when she thought the call would go to voicemail, Cadence picked up.

"Hey!"

"You have some 'splainin' to do, Lucy!" she said in her best Ricky Ricardo impression. Alana had picked that up from watching *I Love Lucy* reruns with her mother. She had always loved Ricky's heavy accent. "I was just thinking about the other night. I don't like being ambushed!"

"Ambushed, Alana? Really? I told you Drew asked me not to say anything."

"What's with him?"

"He was afraid you wouldn't go."

"Since when is he afraid of anything?" Alana sucked her teeth and waved her hand, dismissing the notion.

"Never mind that, missy. How about you explain that tongue duel that the two of you seemed to have gotten lost in at the after-party! Your entire mood changed after that. You even avoided me at the office yesterday and then you left early so I never had a chance to interrogate you. What's going on?"

"I wasn't avoiding you." Alana smiled sheepishly, even though Cadence couldn't see her.

"Hello!" Cadence said after a considerable pause.

"James was there."

"What? Where?"

"At the party. I didn't realize it until just before I pulled Drew onto the dance floor. Do you know that fool looked at me, turned to his date, kissed her and looked back at me again? That's when I—" Alana lowered her voice "—kissed Drew."

"Come again?"

"Ugh! That's when *I* kissed Drew." Alana's voice reached its full volume.

"Alana!"

"Don't scold me, Cay, please! I didn't know what to do. It was stupid. I know. We can be so intelligent in life, but relationships will reduce us to a pile of senselessness." Alana grabbed a handful of her own hair and grunted. "You're not the only one who wanted answers. Drew showed up at my door this morning. He just left a few minutes ago."

"No way!" Cadence sounded shocked.

"Yep. Get this. Drew spotted James staring at me all night. I didn't even know he was there until the party was almost over. Drew sensed that something was up so I admitted that James was my ex. That was so embarrassing!"

"Wow!"

"Yeah. I know."

"I have a question and I want you to be completely honest with me, Alana. Do you still have feelings for James?"

"No. I'm over him. The kiss was a bad idea. I wanted to show him that I had moved on also, but now I have to deal with Drew."

"What do you mean?"

Alana started pacing. "Before he left, he kissed me again, told me he was coming back for me and then walked right out. I stood there dumbfounded for a few moments before I even locked the door."

"Whoa! Maybe that was payback for the other night."

"Here's the problem. When his lips connect with mine, my brain stops working. I can't pull away. I can't believe

I just said that aloud, but it's true. It's like…I can feel every nerve in my body."

"Are you falling for him again?"

"No! Drew Barrington is the last man that I would allow myself to fall for. I told you, I'm done with his kind—with him, period. Besides, he spends most of his time in Europe. A relationship would never work. I wouldn't even waste my time."

"Sometimes we can't control who we fall for."

"Humph. Until I'm ready to get back in the game, I'll stick to my rules. I want someone accessible. Not someone who just wants to flirt, have sex and then walk away for months at a time. I deserve more."

"You're a great woman and your prince is out there somewhere."

"Please! No more frogs!" Alana whined and both of them laughed.

"Hey, I can't promise that!" After a few more moments of laughter, Cadence said goodbye.

Alana finished cleaning up the kitchen and got ready to run her Saturday-afternoon errands. As she headed to her bedroom, her cell phone rang again. Assuming it was Cadence calling back, she ran to the kitchen to grab the phone. Perhaps she had left something unsaid. When Alana saw James's number, she stopped walking and stared at her display.

What does he want? "Hello?" She was going to let the call go to voicemail, but her curiosity got the best of her.

"Hey!"

"Fancy hearing from you. What's up?" She was collected and proud about it.

"It was nice seeing you the other night. You looked great."

"Thanks. What can I do for you, James?" Alana shifted her stance and placed a hand on her hip.

"Listen… I'm sorry about the way things went."

Alana continued to her room and flopped onto the bed. "I just wish you would have picked up the phone or told me face-to-face. I think I deserved more than a text."

James was silent for a few moments and then said, "I guess that wasn't the best way to do it."

"Well. It's done now." Alana wanted to tell him not to do the same thing with his current girlfriend. She also wanted him to know that she was over the whole thing and the best way to do that was to remain unaffected. "Take care, James. I wish you the best." She thought that telling him to have a good life would make her seem bitter.

"Alana!" She heard James yell just as she was about to end the call.

"Yes?"

"Maybe we should meet so we can talk."

"Thanks, but that won't be necessary." *It's too late.* Alana ended the call.

This interaction was confirmation for Alana. James had been a walking red flag that she had blatantly ignored, but she was no longer upset with him. In fact, she was grateful for the lesson. She would only give her all to the man who proved he deserved it.

Despite her proclamation, Drew's words still taunted her throughout the rest of that day.

I'm coming back for you. She recalled his husky voice when he'd said those words and a slight shiver squiggled down her spine.

Chapter 8

Despite the erratic weather across the States this February, Austin was holding at a comfortable sixty degrees. Clear blue skies stretched over the landscape like a canopy. Drew was able to keep the slight bite from the occasional breeze from getting to him with a light leather jacket and riding gloves. The dry ground was perfect for a day at the track. Drew's morning workout had him energized.

"Ready to ride?" Drew's teammate Sean asked as he stepped out of The Charlotte—a boutique hotel that Drew preferred during his visits to Austin. It offered a little reprieve from the fuss of the larger hotels. The two shook hands.

"Ready." Drew beamed. He knew just what he wanted to work on today. Drew was in his element. He pictured himself tightly hugging the track's sharp turns, leaning so close to the ground he could reach out and touch it.

Many relished the speed. Drew enjoyed the other aspects of racing that challenged him the most, like mastering treacherous curves, where skill and technique ruled.

"Sir?" The young valet brought Drew out of his visions of racing grandeur. Drew handed him the ticket, held his face high to catch the cool breeze passing by and scanned what he could see of the city's urban landscape.

There was something about Austin that he appreciated, though he wasn't sure what it was. It had the charm of the south with a cool vibe. It was a hot spot for music lovers of all types. Night offered every possible option to indulge in whatever one was in the mood for. What Drew loved for sure was the fact that Austin was a race-loving town. Just beyond the city's borders was America's only MotoGP track—a US home for the best and fastest racing in the motorcycle world. He wondered if a city boy like him could actually live there.

The valet arrived in Drew's rental. As they drove, the landscape changed from tall buildings jutting toward the sky to cozy neighborhoods and roads both wide and narrow that wound their way through expansive greenery to their destination.

Drew parked and jumped out of the car with Sean by his side. Scores of riders, from novices to professionals, poured into the massive space that spanned over twenty acres with 3.4 miles of racing track, seating for 120,000 fans, an amphitheater, a soaring observation tower and a grand plaza with a promenade featuring retail and concessions shops.

They met the rest of the crew at the entrance. Adrenaline had already begun to pump through Drew's veins. Track days were like long tailgate parties. Music blared from the speakers throughout the stadium, beer flowed, groupies dressed scantily and motorcycle lovers relished in their element.

"Hey!" A lean man with long, slick hair pulled into a low ponytail greeted the team with high fives and brief hugs. His Argentinian accent was thick.

"Antonio! My man!" Drew greeted him and the rest of the team. He was fond of his former team member, who still raced with Hiroshi. He'd taught Drew a lot about technique.

Gary Hayden walked up just as they were about to enter the building. Continuing the greetings, Drew offered him a cool and distant hello, void of all the enthusiasm he exhibited with the other racers. It was obvious that Gary wasn't his favorite person and for good reason. Drew knew he was likely to see him there. The two had fallen out with one another years ago when they had raced in the same division. Since then they cordially kept their distance whenever their paths crossed. Fortunately, they were never on the same team, which would have forced them to set their differences aside. That would have been hard for Drew since Gary wasn't a very likable guy, and his competitive nature extended way beyond the track. Gary had ultimately crossed the line when he had actively pursued Jade Donnelly, Drew's ex-girlfriend, while she and Drew were still together. She had been the one woman that Drew had considered marrying. Drew and Gary had almost come to blows the time Gary had openly flirted with her right in Drew's face before one of their races. Drew's anger almost cost him third place.

The men headed to the locker rooms to put on their gear before heading to the track, where their custom practice bikes were waiting for them. They paid a local instructor to maintain and house their motorcycles.

Sean leaned toward Drew as they walked with their

helmets tucked under their arms. "You and Gary still at odds?"

"I wouldn't consider us as being *at odds*. I'm not fond of the guy and, honestly, he's not fond of me, so I guess we're even." Drew wouldn't say any more on the matter.

Sean shrugged and then nodded. "I guess that's fair," he said after a while.

"You're still coming with us to the community center tomorrow afternoon?" Drew asked Sean, changing the subject.

"Of course."

"Cool." Drew clapped his hands together. "Now let's ride!"

A loud voice saturated with a languid Southern drawl interrupted the country music blaring through the speakers. The second announcer whooped and joined the first with an accent that was just as strong. Hastening at their enthusiasm and instructions, some riders mounted their bikes while others prepared for their turns on the track. The men talked about their expectations for the upcoming season until it was time for them to hit the track.

Drew only half listened, bobbing his head to Tim McGraw as he inspected his bike. His appreciation for his motorcycles rivaled his fondness for his lovers. Drew softly stroked the metal with a mix of admiration and respect. He brushed off a speck of dust and straddled the machine with a sated smile.

"Yeah!" Drew yelled out to amp up his racing brethren.

"Woo!" Sean pumped his fist.

"Hiroshi!" Antonio yelled, cupping his hands around his mouth like a megaphone.

Drew and Sean waved him off with a hearty laugh. Gary simply nodded.

"It's time to ride!" Drew started the engine. He could feel the vibration through his entire body. He closed his eyes to feel it deeper. "You're beautiful, baby." Drew spoke sweet nothings to his bike. He revved the engine. It was almost time for them to hit the track. His heart beat a little faster as he continued bobbing his head to the music. He zoned out the announcer's voice completely now as he focused on Bebe, which was what he called this bike. Each one had a feminine-sounding name that doubled as a nickname for something else. This one was a beast—fast, furious, custom-built to his specifications with a fire-breathing dragon painted on the sides. Pulling his helmet down over his face, Drew took off first, riding slowly toward the starting point.

Drew looked out over the track, taking note of the sharp turns, envisioning himself leaning into them. He was ready to give the new techniques he'd learned a try. Folks in the stands and along the sidelines cheered as if it were an actual race day. Drew revved his engine again, smiling hard behind his helmet. Riding gave him so much joy.

Sean and their fellow racers lined up. The announcer called for the start. Drew leaned forward on the bike, his chest nearly touching the body. He set the bike in gear. Horns blew. With skillful control, Drew released the clutch, simultaneously churned the throttle, picked up his feet and took off.

Drew leaned even closer to the bike.

"Speak to me, baby girl." The bike did, revving, rather whirring, letting Drew know she was ready for more. Drew advanced the bike into the next gear, waited to hear her hum again and then kicked it up one more time. Excitement surged in his core and spread through every nerve in his body. The speed was intoxicating. He wanted more, yet waited for the bike's cue. She purred again and he took the gears up another notch. Despite incredible speed, he felt weightless and free as if he were riding through clouds.

Drew approached his first curve, a minor one for a professional. He leaned toward the ground, pushing his motorcycle in the direction of the curve, squeezing the bike between his legs. He balanced his weight by tilting his upper body in the opposite direction and then guided the bike back into an upright position as he came out of the curve. Drew repeated this technique, adjusting his angle to get the turns just right. Happy with his results, he approached the sharpest turn with fervor. He mastered that fierce turn with precision and then beamed with pride under his helmet. After his first round, Drew challenged himself to cut through the curves cleaner and faster, putting the strength of his upper body to work. There was no doubt he'd gotten better. Nothing could stop him from winning this year.

On his last lap, Drew bolted out of a turn, eating up the track and leaving those around him in his wake. He could feel that someone was gaining on him. Confident and unmoved, he kept his stride and prepared for his next turn. The person behind him came dangerously close. When Drew righted his back after that last turn, he felt a jolt that caused his rear wheel to skip across the pavement. The bike swerved and Drew tried to control it, but he flew several yards in one direction, landing on his shoulder, and the bike went in the other. Drew hurried to his feet and ran to the grass at the center of the track as other bikes whizzed past him. The other racers slowed as a crew ran to Drew's aid while one of the guys from the pit went for the bike. Several riders stopped to see if he was okay. Sean and Antonio were at his side. Medical personnel joined them, asking questions and looking Drew over.

"You okay, dude? I'm sorry, man." The guy who clipped him seemed genuinely worried.

Drew shook his head, shaking off the brief haze from the narrow escape.

"I'm fine," he said. However, his arm hung limp and he held on to his shoulder as pain surged through it. A few gentlemen helped him off the track. The physician on site examined him. There were no broken bones, but his shoulder was dislocated.

At the hospital, they put it back in place and gave him meds. The doctor recommended he follow up with his regular physician.

The pain was bearable after taking the medication that was prescribed, but Drew knew he'd have to care for that shoulder to ensure that it would be strong enough to get through the season. Upset, he cursed. He didn't have time for injuries. Drew didn't want his team to regret signing him. He had a win to secure.

Surprisingly, the next thought that came to mind was Alana. For some reason, he wondered what she might have said had she witnessed his fall. How would she have reacted? He also wondered how it would feel to know that she was in the stands rooting for him. Drew had every intention of finding out.

Chapter 9

Knowing that Drew was out of town helped Alana focus. She needed every bit of her brain to work through her and Cadence's current crisis. Since their practice opened, business had thrived—until now.

Alana pushed herself back from the round table where she and Cadence convened to review the state of their business, drew in a long breath and released it with a groan.

"We need more clients."

"It's not that bad, Alana." Cadence didn't sound too convinced. "We're just experiencing our first lull. It happens in every business. Our financial situation still looks decent."

"I don't want business to be decent. I want our business to flourish and, unless we get more clients, those finances won't continue to be somewhat pretty." Alana stood and walked over to the window overlooking Thirty-fourth Street and folded her arms. She watched as the people below weaved through foot traffic on the wide sidewalks like they were doing a choreographed dance. "We need to be strategic about acquiring clients. With all the work that we put into developing our brand, I don't want us to come across as ambulance chasers. I don't want to find myself stalking newspapers to find out what famous person did something illegal so we can represent them."

"I know." Cadence flopped back in her seat.

"I think we're just spoiled. Most law firms spend years trying to secure the clients who we've represented from the moment we opened our doors."

"I hate to admit it, but being associated with Blake's case put us on the map for those high-profile cases when we opened this practice."

"Exactly. After that, one led to another and we became known for successfully handling famous clients."

"The only problem is—"

"They don't happen all the time." Cadence and Alana spoke at the same time.

"Right." Alana gave Cadence a pointed look. "Truthfully, we don't need a high-profile case. We just need a more steady flow."

"You're right. What tasteful marketing strategies can we use to bring more clients?" Cadence stood and paced, tapping her palm with a pen. "Let's see."

"Oh! I know." Alana opened her journal and started jotting down notes. "I'll have a chat with some of the members at the association who run their own practices. I'm sure they'll have some information that they can share with us."

"That's a good idea. Let's set up a dinner where we can gain some insight into the long term."

"We have a membership meeting coming up next

week. I'll bring it up then. In the meantime, I'll start working on a list of things we can do to get our name out there or perhaps capitalize on the exposure that we received from our last big case."

Cadence rounded the small table and stood behind Alana as she wrote. "Maybe we can hire a PR firm to help us get more coverage like the article that magazine did on us after the Johnson case. It's possible that they can help keep our firm's name in the glow of the spotlight."

"Let's do it!" Alana sat back in her chair and exhaled. "I'm feeling a little better, but I'd feel great if more clients walked through that door." Alana pointed toward the entrance.

"Tell me about it." Cadence looked at her watch. "It's lunchtime. What do you feel like eating?"

Alana reached into her bottom desk drawer, pulled out her purse and stood. "Let's go to the BBQ place on Eighth."

Fifteen minutes later, they were seated at a small table at the rear of the lively eatery, which was filled with impatient patrons trying to get the most out of their lunch hours. After ordering two BBQ-chicken salads, a side of fried pickles and sweet potato fries, they settled into small talk.

"Have you spoken with Drew lately?"

Alana stuck her fork in Cadence's plate and stabbed a sweet potato fry. "Lord, no!" She chewed the fry before continuing. "I haven't heard from him since he left my house that night. Why?"

Cadence cut a strip of her chicken with the side of her fork. "He's been asking about you."

Alana didn't expect her heartbeat to stutter. Her gasp was slight. She cleared her throat to cover her reaction, hoping it went unnoticed, but Cadence's prolonged glance, coupled with a somewhat lifted brow, confirmed that Cadence had heard. Alana sat back and sighed. "Why?"

Cadence put her utensils down and gave Alana a suspicious gaze. "What's really going on with the two of you? Is there something you're not telling me?"

"No. Why would you think that?"

Cadence tilted her head but kept her eyes on Alana.

"Listen, lady—" Alana pointed her fork at Cadence "—you don't have to believe me, but I was serious when I said I wasn't dating." Alana pierced a forkful of salad and swirled it around her plate. Suddenly, she wasn't hungry anymore. "Especially with Drew. I don't have the patience or energy to have a rendezvous with that man. When I start dating again, I want someone who I know will focus on me and me only. Besides, Drew is hardly ever here. I'd never survive a long-distance relationship."

"You don't have to convince me." Cadence held her hands up in surrender.

"And another thing—" Alana pointed again "—this next frog is going to have to put in some major work to win me over."

"Right!" Cadence threw her head back.

"Seriously. From where I stand, they're all frogs until proven princes. Cute frogs, tall frogs, muscular frogs, frogs that break up with you by text and frogs that race motorcycles for a living!"

Cadence leaned back in her chair, holding her belly as she laughed.

Alana couldn't help but join her. "My grandma used to say that if you lie down with dogs you'll wake up with fleas. Well, I say, if you spend time with frogs, you'll end up with warts!"

"Stop! Please!" Cadence begged, still laughing. "I

think Drew has prince potential. If Blake and Hunter could settle down, so can he."

Instead of answering, Alana twisted her lips and filled her mouth with salad, forcing down her food and her smart remark.

"Alana, if Drew pursued you and was truly sincere about being in a committed relationship, would you consider dating him again?"

"Cay, that man probably couldn't spell *commitment*."

"Just answer the question."

"I don't know." Alana shrugged. "I doubt it."

"Aw, I kind of wish things would work out between the two of you. It would be so cool, don't you think? Best friends dating brothers."

"We're not sixteen, lady."

"I know, but it would still be pretty cool, wouldn't it?"

"I guess." Alana looked at her watch. "We'd better get back."

Cadence signaled their waiter for the check just before her phone rang. "Hey, babe!"

A smile that beamed like a sun ray eased across Cadence's face and Alana knew it had to be Blake on the other line. When her facial expression turned serious, Alana became concerned.

What's wrong? Alana mouthed.

"It's Drew," Cadence whispered. "What hospital did they take him to?"

What? When? Is he hurt badly? This time Alana's heartbeat didn't just stutter—it stopped beating altogether for a few moments.

Chapter 10

When Drew saw Alana's number, he picked up right away, reaching for the phone with his good arm.

"What happened?" Panic increased the pitch of Alana's voice.

"Oh, now you want to call me back, huh?" Drew teased as he made his way through the hotel suite into the living room in search of a soda. He favored his left leg as he walked. It was still tender from his fall earlier. Her groan made him laugh.

"I'll assume you're fine. Why did you have to go to the hospital? Did you fall off one of those bikes?"

"Wow! That news went viral. I just called Hunter and Blake when I got back to the room." Drew limped to the sofa, carefully sat and then popped the top on the soda can. "Nothing major. I took a little spill and dislocated my shoulder."

"That sounds major enough to me. How's that going to affect your season?"

"It won't."

"What do you mean, it won't?"

"It has happened before. I have a few weeks before the season starts. I'll be fine by then."

"Are you in any pain?"

"It's just a little sore," he lied. Truthfully, his shoulder ached, thumping like it had its own pulse. He dealt with it, refusing to take any more of the huge pain pills the emergency-room doctor had given him. He needed to be coherent because he still had a race to focus on.

"I'm sure it's not your first fall, but I assume this will keep you off your feet for a while."

"I've dealt with much worse in the past. Broken legs, arms and enough road rashes to cover my body five times over."

"And you still get back on the bike?"

"That's my life, *ma belle!*"

Silence settled across the line for a moment until Alana dismissed herself. "I have to go. I'm glad you're okay though. Be safe."

"Thanks for calling." Drew didn't want her to go. He continued to hold the phone to his ear as she ended the call. A series of beeps indicated that the call was over. Still, he held the phone.

Drew appreciated Alana's concern. Hearing her voice made him want to be near her.

A few days later, Drew booked an early flight that allowed him to make it to midtown by lunchtime. The flimsy sling they gave him at the hospital didn't do much to keep his muscular arm from weighing his sore shoulder down. Adding pain to his injury, the erratic North American climate made his cross-country flight one of the rockiest he could remember. Turbulence shook the plane so violently at one point that Drew had to hold his shoulder to keep it from banging against the chair. By the time he reached Manhattan, he felt like he'd gone a few rounds in the boxing ring.

Drew showed up at Alana and Cadence's building on the west side of Thirty-fourth Street, searched the board for their suite and headed to the fourth floor. As he stepped off the elevator, he nodded approvingly at the modern office space designed for the business world's new class of entrepreneurs. The communal lounge reminded him of a cozy coffeehouse with fully stocked counters where professionals could fill up on caffeine all day. A few people lounged on the sofas tapping away on laptops. Beyond the lounge, there was a large conference room behind glass walls. He walked down the hall toward Alana and Cadence's suite. His limp wasn't as pronounced as it had been the day before. Drew thought it gave his walk a little swagger. He laughed at himself for the thought.

Drew stopped before the large wooden door that bore the name of their law firm, knocked once and twisted the knob.

"Good afternoon, can—"

Drew spread his lips in a sated smile at Alana's apparent surprise. "What happened to my greeting?"

"What are you doing here?" Cadence walked up and hugged him. He winced, hugging her back with one arm.

"When did you get here?" Alana asked.

"What's wrong?" Drew licked his lips. He almost couldn't help it. Alana looked sexy in that simple gray suit. "You're not happy to see me?" Drew opened his arms as much as he could for a hug.

"You and your surprise visits." She allowed him a quick embrace and then stepped out of his reach, but it was enough for her scent to tickle his nostrils and awaken an inkling of desire.

"This is a business. I didn't have to call first," Drew teased. Alana shook her head. "I came to take you two to lunch."

"How's the shoulder?" Cadence asked, clearing the small reception area of random papers.

Drew waved away her concern. "I'm fine." He curled his other arm. Muscles bulged under his short-sleeved button-down shirt. "See that? I'm all man. A little dislocated shoulder can't stop me."

"You're too much." Cadence chuckled. Alana rolled her eyes and shook her head.

"Hey!" Drew pointed his finger at Alana. "If you keep doing that, they're going to get stuck."

Alana gave him a pointed look. Her feistiness was always a turn-on. "You need to take better care of yourself. Is lunch on you?" she teased.

"What kind of man would I be if it wasn't, *ma belle*? Pick the place."

Alana left a note for their receptionist, Jennifer, who was on lunch and they all headed to one of her favorite Asian-fusion restaurants in the heart of the theater district. As expected, the place was filled with demanding professionals and fast-moving waiters trained in getting people seated, fed and checked out in record time.

For a few moments, he watched how skillfully the restaurant staff handled the crowd as he, Alana and Cadence stood by the bar enduring the twenty-minute wait.

"I'll be right back." Drew saw the question in Alana's and Cadence's expressions as he walked away. He left them to wonder.

Drew approached the waif-thin hostess and smiled,

cranking his charm up a few notches. She sheepishly smiled back.

"How can I help you, sir?"

He detected her light French accent.

"Vous parlez français." It was more of a statement than a question.

"Oui!" She smiled again and hung her head slightly.

"Une telle langue magnifique pour une belle fille."

"Merci!"

"No need to thank me for you being beautiful."

She smiled into her shoulders, turning slightly with crush-like glee.

"I'm in a bit of a rush. Would you mind—"

"I'll take care of you. How many in your party?"

Drew smiled again, holding her in his appreciative gaze until she squirmed a little. "Three. My team of lawyers and me." He kept his smile and smoldering eyes directly on her.

She grabbed three menus. "Follow me."

Drew curled his fingers to summon Alana and Cadence, who had been watching his every move.

The hostess placed the menus down and nodded. Drew pulled out chairs for Alana and Cadence before tapping the hostess to get her attention before she walked away. He touched her forearm gently and leaned to her ear. "I'll be sure to share with the management how pleased I am with your service."

She actually giggled. *"Merci!"*

"Vous êtes les bienvenus, Madame."

She nearly floated away from the table. When Drew sat, Alana's and Cadence's eyes were trained on him. Each pair carried a look of suspicion.

Alana untwisted her lips. "I guess flirting gets you everywhere."

"What?" Drew held his hands up innocently. "I didn't want you to have to wait too long to eat."

"I didn't know you spoke French. I'm impressed," Cadence said over the open menu.

"Thanks," Drew answered modestly.

"What else don't we know about you, Drew?"

Drew caught on to Alana's sarcasm, but Cadence put down her menu and looked at him with genuine interest.

"Do you speak other languages too?" Cadence asked.

"Spanish, a little Italian and I can understand German better than I can speak it."

"Wow!" Cadence's eyes grew wide.

"Nice," Alana added.

Drew had work to do with Alana. Wearing down the protective armor around her heart was his mission. He entertained them with his wit as usual. Alana's smile sent signals to his brain, among other places. Drew kept them laughing just to see her pretty lips spread in happiness. He fancied the curves of her breast against her silk shirt.

Drew wasn't quite sure he was ready to settle down, but he did know that when he was, it should be with Alana. After watching her ex eyeing her at the premiere, he knew a woman of her caliber wouldn't stay single for long. Somehow, he had to gain her trust and convince her that something between them could work. Then he'd have to deal with the issue of distance, which wasn't going to change anytime soon.

They ate sushi until they got their fill. Drew hadn't had enough of their company so he convinced them to join him for a drink at a nearby bar before heading back to the office.

"Drew, this behavior is not acceptable on a workday. You've got us out here slacking!" Alana laughed.

"I know. We're supposed to be working on strategies

for attracting clients and researching PR teams who specialize in the legal field," Cadence added.

"Yeah."

"Hey! I didn't force either of you into doing anything."

"The magic words were *your treat*." Alana laughed. "That's hard to walk away from."

"Well, it was also my pleasure. What are you doing for dinner?" Drew eyed Alana, watching her demeanor shift from carefree back to guarded. "And I won't take no for an answer."

Alana groaned. "Sure. Why not?" She'd given in.

Drew smiled. To him that was a signal to move forward.

Chapter 11

Alana had been looking forward to Friday from the moment she walked into her office on Monday morning. As much as she loved having her own business, it was exhausting at times. When she had worked for other law firms, the only thing she had to worry about was winning cases. Now, she and Cadence put in extensive hours to win the cases, pay the bills and keep the doors of the practice open.

Alana planned to stay in her pajamas, snack, read and watch movies for the entire weekend. She'd get back to exercising and hanging out another time. The fact that five o'clock was almost here gave Alana a bit of vigor.

Alana heard a tap on her office door. Before lifting her head, she began waving goodbye, assuming it was their intern, leaving for the day. But then she looked up into Drew's face.

Alana closed her eyes and sighed even though a smile

spread across her lips. He was part of the reason she was so exhausted. Drew had picked her up for dinner after their surprise lunch outing the week before and they'd spent much of their free time together ever since. The past weekend had been a whirlwind of activity from exclusive red-carpet affairs to early-morning runs to pancake breakfasts. It literally took all week for Alana to catch up on her sleep.

Drew never showed up without an adventure.

"I can't!" Alana slowly shook her head.

Drew strolled in and sat on the edge of her desk. "You can't what, *ma belle*?"

Alana both loved and hated when he called her *ma belle* in the perfectly accented way that he did. It sounded beautiful and she loved the special way it made her feel, yet hated that she was so affected by the deep timbre of his voice. Regardless, she had to admit she enjoyed being his friend again. She'd never deny the obvious tension that hovered in the air when they were close to one another, but she felt that she had the strength to fight that. She still wasn't ready to date.

"I'm tired, Drew. I'm going home and staying there all weekend!" Alana shut down her laptop and closed it.

"That's fine with me."

Alana stretched her eyes. "Really?" She didn't believe him.

"Of course. I guess I'll have to give these tickets to Delphine Armah's new Broadway show to someone else."

Alana's eyes popped open wide and her neck stretched forward. "What!" She stood, rounding her desk in an instant. "Are you serious, Drew?"

"Sure am, but if you're tired..." Drew folded his arms across his chest and hummed.

"Don't play with me, dude!"

"I don't play around, *ma belle*." Drew put his hand on his chin. "Hmm. So that also means I'll have to cancel the plans for dinner with the cast after the show."

Alana balked. "Dinner with the… Drew, are you for real?"

His smile taunted her in several ways. "But you're tired. I surely don't want to be a bother."

Alana pursed her lips and squinted at him. "I'll sleep tomorrow. What time is the show?"

"Eight."

"Darn it! I'll be cutting it close if I go all the way home to Long Island and come back." Alana looked down at her suit. "I'd hate to go in this."

"Then let's go get you something to wear."

"You don't have to do that."

"Come on." Drew slid off her desk and grabbed her by the hand.

Alana grabbed her purse and jacket to shield herself from the slight breeze of the unusually warm March day.

"How do you manage to gain access to these things?" Alana wondered aloud.

"What things?"

"Movie premieres, private celebrity parties, shows and dinner with entertainers."

"Oh. I know a guy."

Alana twisted her lips. "Really, Drew."

Drew held out his hand, leading Alana out of the elevator. "Don't worry about it. Just enjoy it all. Let's go get you something to wear."

Drew hailed a taxi and directed the driver to Fifty-seventh and Fifth Avenue. Alana loved those stores but rarely shopped in them. Those price tags didn't lend themselves to weekly shopping on Alana's budget as a fairly new entrepreneur. She saved those shops for very special occasions.

Drew led the way inside one of those upscale shops. A polished clerk wearing a smart red suit, striking red lips, and a neat bun beamed at Drew. The smile on the sales clerk's face indicated how well she knew him.

"Drew! Darling!" She air-kissed him on both cheeks.

"Karen, it's great to see you." Drew embraced her and then placed his hand on the small of Alana's back.

"And who's the lovely lady?" Karen assessed Alana the way a mother would if she approved of a nice girl that her son has brought home for the first time.

"This is my good friend Alana. She needs a nice outfit for tonight. She has exquisite style. Can you help me find something that will make those beautiful brown eyes of hers sparkle even more?"

"You know I can." Karen took Alana by the hand. "Come with me."

Alana allowed Karen to lead her through the shop while Drew took a seat on a contemporary white leather sofa as if he had all the time in the world.

Alana couldn't help but gush just a little. She was reminded of the scene in the movie *Pretty Woman* when Richard Gere took Julia Roberts to those expensive shops along Rodeo Drive.

Alana thought she knew Drew, but lately he'd surprised her. He seemed to be a different person than the guy she dated a few years back. Their dates didn't extend beyond the normal dinner and movie. She was almost afraid that he'd break down her resolve.

Karen set her up in a dressing room and brought a few ensembles. Alana was surprised at how well Karen was able to pinpoint her style. She fell in love with two of the outfits and couldn't decide.

"Drew," Karen called out to him. He looked her way, holding up one finger. With the other hand, he pressed the phone to his ear.

A few seconds later, Drew ended his call, put the phone away and joined them at the rear of the store.

"She needs help choosing, darling," Karen said.

"Give her both," he replied.

"No, Drew, that won't be necessary. Just help me pick something for tonight."

Drew assessed the black jumpsuit as Alana twisted in front of him, showing him how well it fit. It was perfect for a night out on the town.

"You like?"

"I like." Drew nodded.

"Okay, let me show you the other outfit." Alana retreated to the dressing room and returned with a sweaterdress that hugged her in all the right places. She wasn't a gym buff, but none of that mattered in this well-made dress. "What about this?"

From the wide-eyed expression on Drew's face, she didn't have to ask which one he liked best.

"Karen, she'll take both, but please let her wear that one out of the store."

"You've got it, darling."

By the time Alana went back to the dressing room to get her stuff, Drew had already taken care of the bill and Karen had handed him the bag containing the other outfit. Alana put the suit that she'd worn to the store in the bag that Drew insisted on carrying. Luckily, her shoes already went great with the dress. She felt fit to dine with stars.

They headed to the play, which Alana loved. She even cried a few times. Not only was Delphine great, but the entire cast was performed well. When the play ended,

Drew escorted her backstage and she had the chance to meet everyone. They rode together in the limo to a Senegalese restaurant owned by a friend of the director.

Alana tried her best not fidget, but it was hard to keep still when all she wanted was to pinch herself to prove she wasn't dreaming. Delphine and the rest of the cast were diligent about including her in the conversation, yet she still felt as if she were standing outside of herself watching them have dinner with an Academy Award–winning actress and friends. She wondered how Drew had made it all happen—again. Regardless of how it all came together, Alana appreciated how Drew went out of his way to make such memorable experiences possible.

Never without a good story, Drew entertained them with his antics as comfortably as he would have if they had been simply hanging with old friends. She wondered how well he'd known Delphine before today.

Alana knew she was uncharacteristically quiet. Yet she didn't miss the way Drew touched her hand or leg as a way to check in with her. Other times, he'd look to her for confirmation, saying "Right, Alana?" here or there to make sure she was included. She enjoyed being a part of the whole scene. She didn't need to talk.

By the time Drew walked Alana to her door later that night she had to fight every morsel of her resolve to keep from inviting him in for a nightcap. She already knew the regrets she'd scuffle with the next morning so she stood there, facing Drew on her doorstep while the most pronounced sexual tension swirled around them, threatening the very air they breathed. They stood close, drinking each other in without words but communicating in sync—a conversation that was unspoken but understood:

I want to let you in, but I can't—I won't.
I want to come in, but only if you really want me to.

Should we...

Maybe...

But I have my rules...

Alana cleared her throat, snapping them out of their trance. "Good night, Drew."

"Yeah." He cleared his throat too. "Um. Good night, Alana."

They said their goodbyes, but neither moved. A few moments ticked past. Drew leaned over and planted a soft, lingering kiss on her cheek. He stepped back, stared directly into her eyes, leaned forward and planted another on her lips.

Alana closed her eyes. Drew pulled her to him, holding on as if he'd never let go. Alana wrapped her arms around his neck and lost herself in the deliciousness of their kiss. Drew rested his forehead against hers while they caught their breath. Breathing in time, she smiled and he kissed that smile.

Alana opened her mouth and welcomed him again, leading the charge, their tender caresses morphing into greedy gropes that left them panting. Loins ignited, challenging inhibitions. An erection strained against his pants, pressing into and teasing the fire in her belly. They separated from each other, almost abruptly, in order to avoid being completely consumed by their passion and need for one another.

"I'll call you in the morning," he said, respiring and then gently touching her swollen lips with his finger.

Alana knew he would, just like he had every morning since the surprise lunch the week before.

Chapter 12

Drew ended his call with Lucia and headed back to the table with a few of his fellow riders. She had congratulated him on his second-place finish earlier that day and went on to share with him how happy she was with her new boyfriend. Drew had wished her the best, grateful that he didn't have to be the one to cut that string.

Their group captured the attention of every guest in Maderos, a popular Argentinian restaurant, with loud cheers, beer-bottle clinking and infectious laughter. Meagerly dressed groupies trailed them most of the day and sat on the laps of willing riders, joining in the lively festivities. One of those smiling women would have been sitting on Drew's lap if Alana hadn't hijacked his focus. When one voluptuous brunette offered, he politely declined, despite the fact that Alana was more than five thousand miles away.

Drew felt pretty good. Coming in second place in

spite of the bit of soreness that lingered in his shoulder was an accomplishment. He had continued to work on strengthening his upper body over the past few weeks and felt better every day. As he looked toward his third race of the season, he was confident that he could secure a first-place win in the near future.

"We're going to do it again in seven days!" Sean held his wineglass in the air. Cheers rang out again.

"And on my turf," Drew added since the next race, the third of eighteen in the season, was going to be in the United States. "I'm taking home first prize this time, Sean," Drew teased. Sean had come in first today.

"Yeah. We'll see about that," Sean objected.

"Both of you will have to move over," Antonio said in his heavy accent. "I let you both win today, but in America, Antonio takes the trophy!" he said, referring to himself in third person and rolling his *r*s harder than usual because the wine made his tongue lazy.

"Yeah, right!" Drew jutted his chin in Antonio's direction.

"Hey, you come to my country and take the win. I come to your country and take the win. It only seems fair." Antonio's laugh reached the rafters, forcing the others to join in. The atmosphere was too jovial to be in the midst of without being affected.

The blonde sitting on Sean's lap whispered in his ear and he raised his brow at Drew.

"Hey, Sean, make sure you're at the airport on time." Drew knew Sean would be missing for a while if he walked out of the restaurant with that woman.

Sean looked confused. "We leave tomorrow?" His brows knitted.

Antonio laughed. "We've been there before with you

and your…uh…company. Don't get left behind again. We have to be in America by Tuesday."

Recognition flashed across his face. Those who were snickering now laughed heartily, remembering when Sean had taken up with a local woman after one of their races and couldn't be found for two days. His friends always enjoyed reminding him about that.

"Well—" Sean shrugged his shoulders "—she was a great cook."

"I'm pretty sure it wasn't her *cooking* that you couldn't tear yourself away from." Drew raised his glass and sipped his wine. Mid-laugh, he heard his cell phone ring. Drew excused himself and took the call outside.

"Big brother, what's happening?"

"It's Dad." From the tone of Blake's voice, Drew knew something was gravely wrong.

His back became rigid. "What happened?" Desperation seeped into his voice.

"We're not totally sure yet, but it looks like a stroke. Ma just called and they are rushing him to the hospital. How soon can you get home?"

Drew hastened back inside the restaurant with the phone still pressed against his ear. "I'll call you back when I get to my hotel. I'll be on the first bird out of here." Drew had ended the call by the time he returned to the table.

His change in demeanor must have been obvious. The expression on his friends' faces turned serious.

Sean stood, almost knocking over his lady friend. "What's wrong, man?" Antonio stood, as well.

"My dad is being rushed to the hospital. They think he had a stroke. I've got to go."

"I'll come with you," Sean offered.

"Thanks, but I've got this. I'm going to catch the

first flight that's available. See you fellows next week in Texas."

Sean, Antonio and the two other riders hugged Drew and he left. On the taxi ride to the hotel, Drew was lucky enough to book a seat on a flight that was leaving that night. To get to New York, it would take over twenty hours and two layovers, one in Buenos Aires and one in Bogota, but none of that mattered. He needed to be with his family.

Being far away with his dad in crisis scared Drew. He spent the majority of the year at a considerable distance from his family. He prayed that his father would hang on until he arrived the next day and he wished that somehow the time and miles between them could be condensed.

At the hotel, he snatched up his belongings and stuffed them into his suitcase. He'd paid the taxi driver a healthy sum to wait for him. Ten minutes later, he was on his way to the airport. Drew spoke to Hunter, Blake and his mother several times. Since he'd first received the news, nothing had changed. All he knew was that his dad was lethargic and now under the care of the emergency-room doctor at one of New Hope's best hospitals.

Drew got through security with ease but couldn't keep still once he arrived at his gate. He sat for a few moments, stood and then paced. Grabbing his bag again, he strolled through the airport until he found a bar where he stayed drinking native rum. When the rum was unable to quell the angst, he headed back to the gate. Despite all of the people hurrying through the airport, Drew felt as if he were there alone.

Drew's phone rang again. Relieved, he answered right away. He'd become accustomed to feeling a certain level of delight when he heard Alana's voice. It soothed him. That's one reason why he was sure to speak with her several times a week. That and the fact that she'd finally opened up to communicating with him. His plan was to tread carefully until she realized that the two of them together made perfect sense. As hard as it was to be around her and keep his desires at bay, he wanted to make his move at precisely the right time.

"Hey," he said.

"Are you alright? No. Sorry. That was a stupid question. Cadence called and told me what happened. She's at the hospital with Blake."

"I'm fine right now."

"You don't sound fine, but I understand." They listened to each other breathe for a few moments.

"Where are you?"

"At the airport."

"Want me to pick you up tomorrow?"

"Sure."

"Text me the details." The attendant's voice blared through the speakers, announcing that it was time for first-class customers to board. "You've got to go." Alana had apparently heard the woman clearly. "Don't forget to text me. I'll see you tomorrow. Have a safe flight."

Drew ended the call without a salutation. He didn't want to say the word *goodbye*.

Chapter 13

Alana left work early to make sure she'd be on time to pick up Drew at JFK Airport. When she arrived, he was already standing at the curbside with his phone to his ear.

Alana tooted her horn to get his attention.

Drew looked up and then held up his phone. Tossing his bag in the back, he eased into the passenger seat, leaned over and kissed Alana's cheek as if it was their routine. Alana paused for a moment, surprised by the fact that the action didn't feel out of order.

"I was just calling you when you pulled up." He fastened his seat belt. "Thanks for picking me up."

"Where to?"

"The hospital, please."

"I figured that, but I wasn't sure if you wanted to stop at home or my house, at least, to freshen up or something."

"Why? Do I smell?" Drew lifted his arms, sniffed and then laughed.

"No, silly!" Alana laughed.

"A shower would probably feel wonderful, especially since I spent the past twenty-one hours stuck on airplanes, but I need to see my dad." Drew sat back and looked out the window.

After a few moments passed, he cleared his throat but kept his face turned toward the window. Alana allowed him the space to feel without interruption. Silence dominated most of the ride to the hospital. She'd never seen Drew this quiet before.

Alana finally made her way through the slow crawl of evening rush-hour traffic and entered the hospital's parking lot, retrieved a ticket and quickly found a spot. Drew still hadn't said much and hardly looked in her direction. She felt for him—having witnessed her father's health scare a few years back, she understood the angst he was going through. Fortunately, her dad had made a full recovery from his heart attack and changed his lifestyle for the better. Her dad was her superhero and she was sure Drew felt the same way about his father.

Drew stepped out of the car. His eyes appeared strained. Alana wasn't sure if it was from trying not to cry or fatigue from the long flight. She rounded the car and took Drew by the hand—a small gesture to let him know that she was there for him. His smile looked more like a weary frown and he mouthed *thank you*.

Hand in hand, they walked into the hospital and headed to the elevators as they had been directed by the guard. When the elevator doors opened on the second floor, Drew squeezed her hand a little as he stepped off. She could feel his trepidation. It showed in his walk. He slowed as they reached the room in ICU where his father lay. Abruptly, Drew stopped and closed his eyes for moment before taking a deep breath. He looked at

Alana. She nodded. He nodded back. She gave him a warm smile. She understood. Drew didn't know what he was walking into and he needed to brace himself.

After another breath, he slowly moved forward. His mother stood and ran to him the second he hit the door.

"My baby's here! Drew, honey." Joyce looked him over. "Are you okay?" She wrapped her arms around him, shut her eyes and held on.

How sweet, Alana thought. Her husband was lying in a hospital bed connected to tubes and wires that monitored every bodily function and she was concerned about Drew. Alana admired a mother's way of exuding love.

"I'm fine, Ma." When Joyce finally released him, he kissed her forehead. "The question is, how are you?" Drew held both his mother's hands in his. She nodded wearily. After a while, he walked over to his father's bedside.

Joyce opened her arms and Alana stepped in. She hugged her just as long and tight as she had just hugged Drew.

"Thanks for bringing him, sweetheart."

"No problem, Mrs. Barrington."

Joyce walked over, stood beside Drew and rubbed loving circles on his back. Drew had his father's limp hand in his, moving his thumb across the back of it.

"How's he really doing?"

"He's resting now. They have him sedated," Joyce whispered. "He's doing so much better. Fortunately, it wasn't a massive stroke. They hope to have him out of ICU by the middle of the week." Joyce told him about Floyd falling when he had gotten up to go to the bathroom and explained that the doctors said that he was lucky to have had someone there with him. They expected him to recover well, but he'd need several months of therapy to get back to his old self.

Joyce leaned her head against Drew's arm and he placed his head against the top of hers. They stayed that way for several moments, watching Mr. Barrington's chest rise and fall in syncopation with the symphony of hisses and beeps of the monitors. Drew gnawed on his bottom lip. From the tight way his facial muscles were set, Alana imagined him willing himself not to cry. The love that manifested in those simple gestures between mother and son almost brought Alana to tears.

"Sweetie, did you eat?" Joyce finally broke the silence.

"No, I came straight here from the airport."

"Why don't you get yourself something to eat, rest up a little and come back. I'll give you my keys and you can go to the house instead of driving all the way to Brooklyn. You must be tired from racing and then all that flying. I know how that stuff can wear you out. When you come back, you can hang out with him as long as you want."

"Come on, Drew. It will be my treat." Alana was certain that he had to be hungry. Airline food wasn't the most appetizing and he'd been cooped up in those cabins for almost a full day.

Drew leaned over and whispered something in his father's ear before leaving his bedside.

"What about you, little lady?" he asked his mother. "Have you eaten?" Drew massaged her shoulders from behind.

"Oh, I'm fine. People have been bringing me stuff since yesterday. I sent Hunter and Blake home with a bunch of goodies."

"Okay, I'll be back." Drew kissed his mom's forehead.

Joyce squeezed Alana in a warm hug again. "Tell him to get some rest," she whispered in her ear.

As they left, Alana pondered Drew's interactions with his mother. She could draw good conclusions about a man who treated his mother well.

"After we eat, do you want to go to your mother's house or…home?" She stopped herself from offering her place as an option.

"I already appreciate you picking me up at the airport. I don't want to take you out of your way by having you drive me all the way to Brooklyn. Let's just go eat. I'm starving."

"You got it."

They left the hospital and headed to one of Alana's favorite grills in Garden City. The crowd was light as usual for a Monday evening. They were seated right away. Alana ordered wine and Drew ordered a snifter of cognac.

"You seem more at ease than when I first picked you up." Alana ran her finger around the rim of her glass.

"I didn't know what to expect. Being so far away, I automatically thought the worst. I prayed…"

Alana raised her brows at his admission.

"So Drew Barrington prays," Alana teased.

Drew shook his head and chuckled. "I just wanted him to be alive when I arrived. I couldn't wait to get off that plane. Now that I've seen him I know that even though he has a tough road ahead of him he'll still be here. That's all that matters to me. I can't imagine losing my dad. He's like a superhero."

Alana's heart swelled. She knew exactly how he felt. She also appreciated meeting the tender side of Drew. It made him…real.

Conversation came with ease and they enjoyed their food. Back in the car, Alana asked again, "Okay. Where to?"

"How about your house?"

Alana swallowed. "You sure?"

"I don't really want to be alone."

She cleared her throat. "Okay."

It took a quick twenty minutes to get to Alana's house. She led the way to the den, disappeared and returned with a towel and washcloth.

"You know where to go whenever you're ready. I'm going to run upstairs and get out of these work clothes."

"Need some help with that?"

Alana narrowed one eye at him. "Drew," she admonished.

"If you don't want my help, I was only joking, but if you do, then I'm serious."

"Drew!" Alana yelled as she climbed the stairs. His laugh followed her to the room.

Alana removed her suit and slipped into a pair of blue yoga pants and a graphic T-shirt that hung slightly off one shoulder. She stuck her feet into a pair of fluffy pink slippers and came back downstairs.

Drew was no longer in the den and his washcloth and towel were gone. Alana inclined her ear toward the bathroom that adjoined her first-floor guest room and heard the shower running. She retrieved a bottle of wine from the butler's pantry and placed it, along with a glass, onto the tray sitting on top of the center ottoman. She looked around for the remote and placed it on the tray, as well.

Just as she placed a throw across the arm of the sectional, Drew came out of the bathroom.

"I brought you—" Alana turned to find Drew standing in the entrance wearing nothing more than a towel. Moisture caused the creases of his rippled abs to glisten and her core to tighten. "Put some clothes on!" Alana acted as if taking in the masterpiece that was his body had no effect on her. However, the urge to run her hands across his smooth skin and trace the ripples in his stomach made her giddy. The jewel creating an imprint behind his towel beckoned her. Alana turned quickly so she wouldn't get caught staring.

"I just got out of the shower." He stared at her incredulously—arms out and shoulders lifted.

"I know that. Where are your clothes?"

Drew smirked. "Behind you."

"Okay, let me go so you can get dressed." Alana stepped around him, avoiding the sight of Drew's muscular arms. "I put the remote, some wine and a glass on the ottoman for you. That throw is there in case you get cold." She looked at everything she mentioned to keep from considering Drew. Still she noticed how toned his calves were and then, once again, she looked away. Drew walked right up to her.

"Do I make you uncomfortable?"

"Of course not," she huffed. Alana planted her arms on her hips and her eyes on the blank TV screen.

"Alana." Drew touched her chin, guiding her head in his direction. Her pulse quickened and her mouth ran dry. "I hate to think that I make you uncomfortable."

She pulled away from his touch but could still feel him.

"You don't." She walked away. "I'll give you a moment to get dressed."

A while later, Alana returned. Drew had on sweats and a T-shirt. She held car keys in her hands and jingled them. "Feel free to take my car if you want to go over to the hospital anytime tonight. I just need to get to the train station for work in the morning."

Drew's smile and nod expressed his appreciation. "Come." He patted the space on the sofa next to him.

Alana shifted her weight to one foot, folded her arms across her chest and tapped the floor with her other foot.

"I won't take a bite out of you, unless you want me to."

"Drew."

"I'm kidding. Jeez!" Drew shook his head. "Now, come. Sit."

Alana dropped her arms like an exasperated teen and trudged over to the sofa. She plopped down. Her expression remained cool while Drew laughed. His laugh made her laugh.

"You're trouble, you know."

Drew simply shrugged. He didn't deny or confirm that he was something to be reckoned with. He took her hand. "I just want to thank you for today. I appreciate everything you did." He swept his hand toward the wine and glass. "And all you're doing. Thank you." His sincerity cooled her demeanor.

"You're welcome."

"Watch TV with me."

Alana took a deep breath.

"I'll behave. I promise." Drew slid his lips into one of those sexy smiles that she could never read. She didn't know if he could be trusted or not. Worse, she didn't know how long she could trust herself with Drew in her home.

She snatched the remote from him. "If I'm going to watch TV with you, then we're going to watch what I want to watch."

"I love it when a woman takes the lead." Drew ducked, knowing that a swat was on its way.

Alana sat back on the couch and flipped through the channels until she found one of those cable networks that played reruns of *Law and Order* all day long.

"I'm cool with that." He lay across the couch, resting his head in Alana's lap. She looked down at him. He was such a tease.

"What?" he asked innocently.

"Just watch the TV, silly," she instructed. Alana caressed his closely cut hair, gently scratching his scalp.

Drew's eyes lazily closed halfway. He seemed to enjoy the soothing gesture. Drew looked up at her and winked. Alana smiled back, leaned forward and kissed his lips. Drew sat up, slid his arm around her neck and brought her closer. The exchange was warm, sensual and passionate, ending with countless kisses.

Drew laid his head across her lap again and laced one hand in hers. With the other, she continued caressing his head until Drew's eyes grew too heavy to keep open.

Carefully, she lifted his head from her lap and eased up. She covered him with the throw, lowered the volume on the TV and changed to a music channel that played soft jazz. Dimming the lights as she exited the room, she softly said, "Good night."

Thoughts of all the possibilities with Drew accompanied her to the bedroom. Maybe they could become something. Perhaps she might consider giving him another chance. She tried, albeit unsuccessfully, to deny her attraction to him, which now grew much deeper than just the physical. Could he be worth breaking her rules? Things were certainly different this time around. Drew was more compassionate, more attentive. Could he give Alana what she'd always sought? Could he actually become her prince?

Alana turned those thoughts and the vision of Drew's freshly showered body over in her mind. She pictured him sheathed only in a towel. She didn't want to think about how scrumptious he looked—didn't want to remember all the delicious things he could do with what was hidden under that towel—but her memories betrayed her. Then she remembered how tenderly he dealt with his parents. That made her smile—even though she didn' want to. Memories like that were detrimental to her rules

Chapter 14

By the time Alana woke up the next morning, Drew had showered and was in the kitchen preparing breakfast to the rhythms of '90s R&B.

"Hey."

Drew looked up and smiled. Alana couldn't know how sexy she looked in a smart blouse, black trousers and pumps. She might as well have been prancing around in a negligee as far as he was concerned. It would have been equally arousing. "Good morning!"

"You made all of this?" She looked around in awe.

"My token of appreciation. Thanks for yesterday." Drew placed eggs, turkey bacon and biscuits on a plate. He placed a small jar of organic peach preserves that he'd found in her refrigerator next to the plate and poured orange juice in a wineglass. He presented the meal with a grand sweep of his hand. *"Bon appetit!"*

Alana sat and scooted her chair closer to the table. "It

looks delicious. Thank you." Closing her eyes, she said a quick grace and then paused. "I had biscuits in the fridge?" She looked confused.

"No."

Alana cast him a sideways glance. "Then where did these biscuits come from?"

"I made them." Drew plated his own breakfast as he continued bopping with the music.

"You *made* them?"

Standing erect, Drew put his hand across his chest, acting as if he were offended. "Yes. I *made* them."

Alana took a bite, closed her eyes and moaned. "No way," she said, still chewing.

"I'm great at a lot of things, remember?" He paused to let the innuendo settle as he sat. When she shook her head at him, he laughed.

"You're so damn fresh." Alana giggled.

"Mom taught us all a few family recipes. She said it didn't matter that we were boys. We needed to know how to cook."

"So good," she said with her mouth full. "Did you get back to the hospital last night?"

"No."

"I didn't think so. Jet lag," she said and he nodded in agreement. "You can take my car today if you want."

"I appreciate that." Drew spread preserves on his biscuit.

"Just drop me off at the station so I can catch my train into the city. I'll show you where to leave my keys when you're done."

"I'll have my mom, Hunter or Drew follow me back. They'll take me to Brooklyn." Drew wanted to spend more time with her but knew she needed to get to work.

She'd already voiced her concerns about building her client list. "Are you busy this weekend?"

"The usual errands. Why?"

"This weekend's race is in the States, right outside of Austin. Blake and Hunter were coming out for it, but now, with Dad being in the hospital, they're going to stay here. I'm coming right back when it's over. Have you ever been to a motorcycle race before?"

"Nope." Alana took the last bite of the biscuit, wiped her mouth and pushed her plate back. "I've never known much about it until I met you."

"Would you like to come?"

Alana waited a moment before she answered. "I guess." She shrugged.

"Great. I'll take care of everything. You'll enjoy it."

Alana looked at her watch. "We'd better get going so I can catch my train."

Alana reached for her plate and Drew held his hand out. "I'll do that. Get yourself ready."

Alana looked at him with a brow raised.

"I got this," he reassured her.

"Okaaay…" Alana looked puzzled. Slowly, she turned and headed upstairs to get her shoes and handbag.

Drew understood her confusion perfectly. She'd never seen this side of him. He hadn't taken Alana as seriously as he should have when they had first dated. Now he was hitting the Restart button and coming from a new angle. He needed to dispel the myths he'd help create and guide her to realizing that he was good for her.

"Okay. I'm ready," Alana announced as she descended the stairs moments later.

Drew was heading toward the door just as she made it to the bottom step. He paused to allow her space to walk in front of him. He watched her hips sway in those well-fitting pants as she grabbed her coat and sauntered through the front door. He loved the way she strutted in heels.

Drew opened the passenger side door and examined her as she climbed in before he rounded the car to the driver's side. He chuckled at the notion of living this kind of *normal* life, having breakfast and heading to work in the morning with your partner. He'd never played house before. Most of the time, he avoided spending the night, but there was something about this kind of routine with Alana that felt right—even if it had only been one night.

Drew also appreciated her display of selflessness— the way she supported him in recent weeks and how she consistently asked about his shoulder until he finally told her it was all healed. None of the other women he spent time with showed him that much concern.

Drew and Alana chatted during the several minutes it took to get her to the commuter train station. Pulling up to the drop-off area, he put the car in park and turned toward her.

"What?" she questioned him. He simply smiled. "Why are you looking at me like that?"

"You're a beautiful woman."

Alana cleared her throat. "Thanks." She sat coyly with her eyes cast downward as she fiddled with the handle of her bag.

"Oh, now you're shy?" Drew teased.

"Whatever, Drew." Giving him a quick peck, Alana pulled the door handle to get out.

Drew grabbed her arm to stop her. When she turned, he leaned toward her and kissed her lips. Bringing her closer, Drew slid his hand behind her head and deepened the kiss. Her hand rested on his chest. When Drew finally released her, he had kissed her breath away.

Alana exhaled slowly. Drew sat back, giving her a moment to collect herself. She licked her lips, which made him smile.

"I need to catch my train." She stepped out of the car and leaned over into the open window. "I'll see you later."

"Have a good day." Drew's eyes followed her up the escalator and onto the platform before he took off. He was getting closer.

Drew drove to the hospital feeling rejuvenated and optimistic. When he arrived, his mother was sleeping in a chair and holding his father's hand. Quietly, he stood by his father's side, watching his chest steadily rise and fall. His mother stirred.

"Hey, baby." His mother stood. Drew kissed her forehead and hugged her.

His father's eyes fluttered. Drew turned to him.

"Dad."

Floyd tried a smile. His mouth opened, but no words came out.

"Don't try to speak."

Floyd nodded slightly. Drew's chest filled with air. Overwhelmed by the sight of his father's smile, he took his hand and squeezed gently.

Feeling better about the state of his father's health, Drew pulled up a chair, turned on the TV and spent the rest of the morning and afternoon soaking in his parents' presence.

Chapter 15

Alana couldn't believe that she was actually on her way to Texas to be with Drew for the weekend. He'd left two days earlier to get ready for the race. Drew had never made it to his home in Brooklyn. He'd split his time between his father's bedside and Alana's house. They'd shared a few more breathtaking kisses, but he hadn't attempted any level of intimacy beyond that. Alana couldn't honestly say that she'd deny Drew if he had tried. She was experiencing a completely new Drew—a version that was becoming harder to resist. This Drew doted on her, made breakfast, lunch and dinner some days. This Drew gave hello and goodbye kisses. This Drew fell asleep across her lap and held her hand for no reason at all. This Drew spent days with her without trying to bed her. This Drew was beating down her defenses with every gentlemanly gesture and she wasn't sure she was happy about it.

Alana had initially declined his offer to join him in Texas, but he refused to accept that. She finally relented when she received her flight itinerary and hotel reservations at the Four Seasons by email. This Drew was also insistent and presumptuous, two traits she did recognize as belonging to the Drew whom she'd always known. Cadence told her she'd be a fool to not go. Neither of them had taken time off since they had started their practice almost a year and a half ago. Time off was overdue.

Alana was booked on the first flight out, giving her a full day when she arrived in Austin. Drew advised her that he wouldn't be able to see her until later that day since he was going to be attending meetings with the Delgado team as well as completing the testing and qualifications that were required before each race. She planned to kick back during her free time. She'd downloaded several books on her e-reader and planned to get a massage.

On her way to claim her baggage, she was met by a pudgy gentleman in a black suit holding a sign with her name scribbled across it. He seemed to have known who she was before she confirmed it.

"Pleasure to meet you, Ms. Tate." The mature man smiled and nodded warmly. "I hope your flight was wonderful. Let's get your luggage, and we will be on our way."

She nodded back. "Thank you—"

"Harry, ma'am."

Alana noticed his heavy Texan accent, which was more obvious in those two words than it had been in the several sentences he'd said previously.

She smiled. "Thank you, Harry."

Harry stepped aside to let her go first. Several moments later, a light flashed and the belt began to move bags of all shapes and sizes past them. Alana's bag was one of the last to come out—possibly because it was one of the first to be loaded onto the plane back in New York. She'd arrived at the airport rather early.

Harry grabbed her suitcase and led her to the limousine. Making sure she was comfortable, he offered water before driving off.

"I recognized you right away, Ms. Tate. You're even prettier in person."

"Thanks. Did you see a picture of me?"

"Sure," he sang. "Mr. Barrington told me to take good care of you too. I promised I would."

Alana closed her eyes and smiled. Their last kiss came to mind, and she could almost feel it. She moaned low in her throat. Her eyes popped open. Alana looked up front to make sure Harry hadn't been watching. He was busy humming a jovial tune. He drove slowly onto the expressway. It was a good thing she wasn't in a rush. Drew was slipping inside of her forbidden territory. Alana was supposed to be protecting her heart, using her rules as her security brigade. She needed to get a handle on herself before things went too far.

After this weekend, she was going pull back from Drew. With his racing season in full swing and his father in the hospital, it wouldn't be hard to avoid him. This weekend would be their grand finale.

Harry broke into her thoughts, offering a history lesson about the city as he exited the expressway. The rest of the ride to the hotel was a guided tour, piquing Alana's interest about the trendy city. Harry spoke affectionately of Austin, his hometown, as if he was beating his chest with pride. When they arrived at the hotel, Harry delicately handed her over to the accommodating hotel staff, bid her a wonderful trip and told her he looked forward to seeing her later. Alana wasn't sure why she'd see him later but smiled politely as she thanked him and tried to put a tip in his hand.

"Oh no, Ms. Tate. All of that has been taken care of—quite handsomely, might I add." He tipped his hat. "Enjoy your stay."

"Thank you, Harry." Alana could get used to this special treatment.

Inside, she quickly checked in and headed to her room with a bellhop at her side. She opened the door and gasped. The suite was massive and elegantly decorated with an amazing view of the banks of Lady Bird Lake. In the center of a living room, there was a round, wooden table with an exotic spray of flowers with her name hanging from a bow. Slowly, Alana approached the table, noticing chocolates and chilled wine with an envelope bearing her name.

"Will there be anything else, ma'am?" The bellhop's voice reminded her that she wasn't alone.

"Oh. No, thanks. One moment." Alana reached for her purse.

"That's okay, ma'am." He held up his hand, nodded politely and exited.

Alana turned back toward the table and picked up the envelope. Carefully, she slid her finger under the flap and pulled out a card that had a beautiful white lily drawn on the front. It had to be a coincidence. Had Drew paid enough attention to know that lilies were her favorite flower?

Inside the card, Drew had written a note. She couldn't wait to see him later either. Telling herself otherwise would have been a lie. Alana walked over to the wall of windows and peered at the city. The clear skies were inviting and summoned her to come out. Alana rolled her suitcase toward the bedroom and propped it up on the luggage stand. The bedroom was as elegantly decorated as the living area. The bed made her think of Drew.

Abruptly, she turned and tramped through the suite in search of a second bedroom. There was none.

"Oh, Mr. Barrington! You don't think you're staying in this room with me this weekend?" she asked shaking her head. She started back toward the bedroom.

Second-guessing her decision to come to Austin, Alana plopped on the bed and fell back. Would she really be able to resist Drew if he came on strong? She had to. With new resolve, she stood. "I'm not going there with you, Drew." She shook her finger and spoke as if he were right in the room and then opened her suitcase.

While sifting through her clothes, there was a knock. She had all of her bags and wondered who could be at the door.

"Just a minute." She peeked around the door before pulling it completely open. Two women stood smiling.

"For your service," the taller one with the jet-black bun said with a slight bow before she stepped past Alana into the room.

"Service?" Alana instinctively scratched her head and watched the two waltz inside.

"Yes. Is here fine?" The shorter woman directed her question to the taller one. She answered with a nod and the shorter woman set up a massage table right next to the windowed wall where the sunlight poured in the brightest.

"What service is this?"

"You are—" the taller one looked at her clipboard "—Ms. Tate?"

"Yes. I am."

"We have you scheduled for a massage, spa pedicure and manicure."

"Oh, you do?" Alana dipped her chin and raised a brow. "Then let's get this party started. Where do you want me?"

For the next hour and a half, Alana took in the lavish comforts of her treatments and the soothing sounds of water fountains. The masseuse drew the sheer curtains and lit several candles. By far, it was the best massage she'd ever had. By the time they were done, room service had arrived. Alana lifted the cover off the plate, threw her head back and laughed aloud. Of course, she preferred a burger over a salad and, on cue, her stomach growled. Alana sat facing the beautiful view as the ladies cleared the massage area and she ate her delicious burger. The meat was tender and juicy. She had to tap the corners of her mouth after every bite.

Once she'd eaten her burger and drank her sparkling water, she sat back wondering what would come next. The knock on the door was sure to answer her question. Alana lifted herself from the sofa and strolled to the door. An attendant handed her another envelope, nodded politely and walked away.

Alana grinned and shook her head. Closing the door, she slid open the envelope, now enjoying the game. There was another card with Drew's scratchy handwriting. Alana was lucky to be able to decipher the messages. This time, Drew told her to enjoy the sights and make sure she stopped by a certain shoe store to pick up some flats in case she hadn't brought any. He ended with noting that he looked forward to their meeting at sunset.

Alana scrunched her brows. "Flats?" She wondered why.

Harry was waiting for her when she reached the hotel lobby. Alana hit the shops on Second Street and East

Sixth Street and found the shoe store on Congress Avenue, where she bought not one but four pairs of sandals.

After Alana had spent hours perusing the downtown area and shopping, Harry ushered her back to the car. "We've got to head back now, ma'am."

"Why, Harry?"

"I can't tell you that." His laugh was big and full and shook his shoulders and his belly. Harry's laugh beckoned Alana to join in.

Back at the hotel, Harry opened the door and told her they would be leaving for her next stop in exactly thirty minutes.

In the room, there was a fresh bottle of wine chilling on the round table. A new note told her to dress comfortably, bring a light sweater and wear the flats. Alana giggled as she put her bags away and changed. She was back downstairs in twenty minutes, filled with a wondrous sense of anticipation. She knew it was time to see Drew and now she couldn't wait. When Harry took her hand and led her into the car, she felt as if she were going to prom all over again.

During the ride, Alana called Cadence. "You won't believe this." She shared her entire day.

"Are you kidding me? This is Drew Barrington we're talking about, right?"

"I know. I can't lie, Cay. He's been so sweet and considerate that he is really starting to look a lot less froggy to me."

Cadence's cackled. "You'd think so after all of this. How romantic."

"Yeah, I guess it is romantic. No one has ever done anything like this for me before."

"Well, you deserve it."

Alana became silent.

"What's wrong, Alana?"

"In the past few weeks, I've seen sides of Drew that I'd never seen before. I don't want to get excited just for him to walk away again. I don't need another frog notch in my belt. Part of me wants to see where this will go, hoping that it works out, but there's another part of me that's a little scared and wants to pull away."

"Aw, I understand. Just have fun. Don't think about it."

"I mean, what can really come of Drew and me? He spends nearly nine months out of the year away. How would I know if I could trust him?" Alana's fear spoke for her.

"You won't know unless you try. Blake and I were talking about this the other day. Drew really seems sincere. Even his brothers are surprised."

"Here we are." Harry's announcement cut through Alana's conversation.

Alana looked around. She didn't see anything but trees. "Hold on, Cay." She looked around again. "Where is *here*?" she asked Harry.

"Your last stop for the evening."

Harry got out, rounded the car and opened Alana's door.

"What's going on?" Cadence asked.

"I have no idea. Harry has driven me to some remote area way behind God's back. What is Drew up to this time?"

"What do you see?" Cadence asked.

Before Alana could answer, she spotted Drew walking from a structure that resembled a hangar. Heat pooled in center of her core. His ruggedly sexy gait carried him toward her on a smooth cloud. A freshly trimmed goatee framed luscious lips that gave her pause as she instantly remembered how they felt.

"Alana." She heard Cadence call her name. She sounded as if she were far off in the distance.

Alana had been besieged by the sight of Drew confidently strutting her way, his taut chest strained against his T-shirt. His light leather jacket gave him an edgy appeal.

"Alana!"

"What?" she responded to Cadence's shout, startled.

"What's going on?"

"Drew's here. I'll call you back."

"You better." Cadence ended the call.

Drew walked up and kissed her. "Did you enjoy your day?"

"Yes," she answered breathlessly as if he'd done more than give her a peck on the lips.

Drew took her by the hand. "Good. Let's go watch the sun set."

Drew walked Alana across a large field. She was so caught up that she didn't notice the hot-air balloon until they got closer. A woman greeted them with flutes of champagne. A gentleman walked up and introduced himself as the pilot and a few others as the crew. He gave Alana and Drew a few instructions and then they signed waivers before climbing into the basket of the air balloon with the woman and pilot.

Alana nervously clung to Drew. He rubbed her hand reassuringly. "You're okay with this?"

"Yes. Just a little nervous."

The balloon was fired up. The ground crew held the balloon until the pilot gave them further instructions. As the balloon ascended majestically above the treetops, Alana became less and less nervous until she was shrouded with a serene sense of peace. Drew never let her hand go.

It was quiet up there, allowing Alana to absorb the

stillness. She closed her eyes momentarily as they soared higher. She opened them to find Drew smiling at her. He lifted his arm and she stepped into the crook of it, nestling against his side. They drank champagne, but being in Drew's arms proved more intoxicating.

"Look at that." Drew pointed to the sun changing colors as it lowered toward the horizon. He held Alana's hand in his.

"Isn't it beautiful?" Alana slowly took in the fresh air as she admired the picturesque sky.

"Are you enjoying this?"

"Drew, this is amazing. I've always wanted to do this. It's one of the things on my bucket list."

"We'll have to take a look at that list and see what else I can scratch off with you. What else have you dreamed about doing?"

Alana paused for a moment. "Having a relationship like my parents' and a family of my own."

"Lots of kids?" he asked.

"A few."

"Hmm." Drew nodded.

"What about you?"

"I've always wanted a little girl who I could spoil. I imagine being wrapped around her little finger."

"Really? That's sweet. I guess I never really thought about you wanting kids with you being a racer and all."

Drew looked directly into Alana's eyes. "With the right woman, anything is possible. I don't plan on racing forever."

Alana's cheeks burned. Could she be the right woman?

After a while, the pilot directed their attention to the sunset again. Alana had never seen one so stunning. She wished they could stay there in the balloon, taking in the splendor of God's evening performance forever.

Once the sun fully set, the pilot landed the balloon. They ended up in a different location, but there was a car waiting, which they called a chaser to take them back to the area where they had boarded the balloon. Their driver Harry was ready for them when they returned.

They drove through the blackness of Texas. By the time they arrived back at the hotel, she'd forgotten to be upset with Drew for assuming that it was okay to set her up in a room with only one bed. She hadn't even asked where he planned on sleeping. She was still caught up in the magnificence of her day. Instead of going straight to the room, they spent some time at the bar, sipping cocktails, holding hands and talking more about their dreams. Alana found herself giggling. She considered putting distance between her and Drew, but she had to admit that she was smitten. Drew doting on her in this way was new and wonderful.

"You're probably tired," Drew said as they headed to the room. "I'll see you in, and I'll be back early in the morning." He kissed her in the open door.

"You'll be back?" Alana was puzzled.

"Yeah."

"Where are you going?"

"To my room."

Alana was disappointed, but she was supposed to be relieved. She cleared her throat. "Where's your room?"

"Right next to yours." He pointed to his door.

"Oh, okay."

"Good night," Drew said but didn't move.

"Good night," Alana said after a moment. Drew's sultry gaze was like a laser that set her insides on fire. "I'll see you in the morning."

Drew stayed there and licked his lips. They sparkled in

the moonlight shining through the window. Alana wanted
to feel them again.

"Bye," she said again before slowly stepping back.
She closed the door, cutting through the rising temperature around them.

Behind the door, Alana panted. She dropped her forehead into her hands. Why was she upset that he wasn't
staying in her room? Her heart thumped. She'd only
closed the door seconds ago and missed him already.

Alana walked circles around the living area, fighting
the desire to run after him. Trying to busy herself, she
went to the bedroom and turned on the TV, filling the
space with background noise. She brushed her teeth and
changed her clothes. It was well past ten, Texan time,
which meant it was past eleven, New York time. Alana
had been up since four thirty that morning. She was exhausted yet couldn't sleep. She texted Cadence pictures
of the sunset from the balloon ride. Cadence expressed
her awe with emoticons.

Why am I fighting this? she thought to herself, but
couldn't answer. Alana stood, grabbed her key and left
the room before she could talk herself out of it.

At Drew's door, she knocked softly. He opened immediately. He had been waiting.

Chapter 16

Drew yanked the door open, cupped her head in his hands and covered her lips with his. The taste of her incited a wild hunger; it was sweet and hot—decadent in the most indulgent way. They moved together, him stepping back, her moving forward. Their lips never parted. They danced that dance all the way to the bed in his room.

Drew pulled back for a moment and searched her eyes. Her kiss-swollen lips parted, begging for more.

"Only if you want this."

Alana nodded.

"I need to hear you say it."

"I want this."

Greedily, Drew devoured her lips, pressing his rising erection against her belly. He scooped her up, carried her to the bed and gently laid her down. Hastily, they tore off each other's clothes. Drew revered her naked body as if it were a rare piece of fine art. Caressing her skin, he drew a line from her neck, around her breast and down to her navel, and then kissed that blazing hot trail.

Alana squirmed beneath him. Drew dipped his tongue in her warm mouth. They could scorch water with the heat emanating from their skin. Alana reached between his legs and held his thickness. Drew hissed and almost bucked but took control. This had to be right. He wanted to satisfy the depths of Alana. He was still proving himself and needed her to know that he didn't just want her. He needed her. They'd had sex before, but today he intended to make love to Alana and leave an indelible imprint on her soul.

Drew slowed their rhythm down, instead taking his time to cater to her whims. He reacquainted himself with her body, exploring her with his fingers and tongue. He spread her legs and then dipped, teased and prodded, paying special attention to every gasp then repeated those actions that seemed to satisfy her the most. He explored other ways to cause her to expel pleasure and pushed those buttons until she was a symphony of pure bliss.

He strummed her bud until her moans and hisses became staccato squeals leading into one elongated cry. Her body bucked. Muscles spasms prevented her ability to move momentarily. Her back bent into a high arch and shook violently. Drew sheathed himself and entered her while her body was still quivering. Her walls tightened around him, threatening to send him to an early release. Drew moved with controlled intent, extending his impending climax. He wanted her to have her fill. He'd never get enough.

Drew leaned forward and kissed her, letting her taste her own sugariness. Wrapping his arms around her, he pulled her snugly against his chest and drove himself deep inside of her. Each stroke was long, purposeful and calculated. She whimpered and her eyes rolled back. He pushed himself into her depth and stayed put for a moment, pausing to collect himself. He started again, rotating his hips to reach every part inside of her. She hissed again, grabbing his back, her hands slipping from the moisture collecting there.

Drew continued a steady, luscious rhythm until he could no longer control his tempo. He drove himself into her faster until his ability to maintain a composed pace completely evaded him. Drew's moan rose from the pit of his core. His stride increased. Alana met him stroke for stroke. She chanted his name frantically, grasping at him. The sweet melody of her desperate pleas sent him over the edge. She joined him there. She screamed. He growled as his release blasted through him, paralyzing him temporarily, holding his rigid body hostage. Empty, he melted onto Alana, rolled over, kissed her forehead and held her in his arms until her convulsing ceased. They found themselves in that very position when the light of the sun nudged them awake the next morning.

Alana rolled away from Drew, attempting to ease out of the bed.

"Where are you going?"

"Oh…um. Back to my room."

"Why?"

"Drew." Alana sighed.

Before she could say another word, he held his hand up. "Don't say this was a mistake."

Alana looked away.

Drew sat up. "It's a mistake when you don't care about the person you just made love to."

"It was sex." She still hadn't looked at him.

"Really?" Drew huffed. "Did it feel like just sex to you?" he asked.

Alana didn't respond. Instead she closed her eyes. Drew wondered if she was trying to wish him away. He moved closer to her.

"What's the problem? Why do you keep pushing me away?" Alana kept quiet, but Drew refused to let her off the hook. "Why are you fighting this?"

"There's nothing to fight. It's not like we're dating or anything."

That felt like a hit in the groin to Drew, but she was right. They had never established anything between them. Still her answer wasn't good enough.

"Why are you fighting this, Alana?" he repeated adamantly.

"I don't want to get hurt again." Alana stood, holding the sheets against her naked body. "You've been so wonderful that I forget how bad it hurt when you left me to go back to your ex. I was fine when you weren't around, but every time you returned to the States, I remembered what it felt like. For a long time, I was scared to take chances with my heart. Then James came along and I finally let myself fall in love just to be hurt again. Falling for you scares me to death."

"You think I'm going to hurt you?" Drew looked at her incredulously.

"I know you will." Alana covered her body and walked over to the chair where some of her clothes had been tossed from the night before. "I'm sorry. I shouldn't have come over here last night."

For a moment, Drew was at a loss. He rubbed his face in frustration. He couldn't remember ever being speechless. However, he understood the reason Alana doubted him, which is why he was working so hard to reverse his reputation.

Drew walked up behind Alana and gently caressed her arm. She flinched. He hated the fact that his touch caused that reaction from her.

"Sorry," he said.

She nodded.

"Can we sit down and talk?" Drew waited for her approval. Several moments passed before she nodded again.

Delicately, he took the clothes she'd gathered from her hands and led her to the side of the bed. Alana continued looking at her hands as he sat next to her. Drew lifted her chin.

"Alana," he said softly.

She lifted her eyes until they met his.

"You don't trust me."

Alana opened her mouth to speak. Drew was sure she'd attempt to object. He put a finger to her lips. "That wasn't a question and I understand why. I haven't shown you the most trustworthy behavior—until now."

Alana averted her eyes once again.

"I also know that you've been hurt and I know what it's like to want to protect your heart, but, in case you haven't noticed, I'm trying to show you another side of me."

She finally looked at him.

"I didn't have the best reputation, but I also didn't have any reason to change my ways. I'm just asking that you give this thing a try."

Alana shook her head. "I don't know, Drew." She averted her eyes again.

"I also need you to be honest."

"About what?"

"What's so scary about me?"

Alana sniffed out a small laugh. "You really want to know?"

"I wouldn't have asked if I didn't."

"Fine." Alana turned toward him for the first time. "You run from commitment. You don't take women seriously, and I'm sure that you probably have a different woman in every city." Her reasons rolled off her tongue with such ease that Drew was slightly taken aback.

Drew tilted his head in agreement. "Okay, you got me." He laughed. Alana swatted him. He ducked, but she still grazed his arm.

"I won't run from you. I take you very seriously and you're the only woman I want in any city."

Alana's eyes widened. Her mouth fell open. "What are you saying, Drew?" she asked.

Instead of answering, Drew locked her in his gaze, leaned forward and kissed her. She seemed to melt under his touch, so he pulled her closer and kissed her deeper.

"I'm saying that I won't take no for an answer. I want to be with you, Alana."

She hugged herself as if the room were cold. "What about the distance? You're traveling most of the time. I don't know if I can handle a long-distance relationship. I want someone who I can touch and feel all the time."

"Being away from you won't be easy. Trust me, I already know." Drew didn't miss the fact that her breath caught at his words. "I'm willing to believe we can work anything out if we want to. Regardless of how far apart we may be at times, I want you to know that your heart is safe in my hands."

Drew noticed the tension leave Alana's shoulders. He wrapped his arms around her and rolled her onto her back. He lifted himself over her and searched her face.

Drew examined her doe eyes, sweetheart lips and high cheeks.

"You're so beautiful," he heard himself say.

She blushed and he kissed each part of her that he'd just admired. He lowered and kissed her nipples. They pebbled and he felt her skin grow warm under his touch. Drew continued, leaving a trail of moist lip prints all the way to her toes and back to her waiting lips.

Last night, they'd made love with urgency. Today, Drew planned to take things deeper than they'd ever gone before.

Chapter 17

Alana entered the office with a bounce in her step and a hum on her lips. She hadn't realized that Cadence was following her until she sat, dropped her purse in the bottom file drawer and lifted her head. Cadence stood at the entrance of Alana's door with her arms folded across her chest and one brow lifted.

"What?" Alana asked.

"You tell me." Cadence took the seat on the opposite side of Alana's desk and rested her elbow on the cherrywood desk. "And don't leave out a single detail."

Alana laughed aloud. "How much time do you have?"

"Oh goodness. That much happened?"

"He got me, Cay."

Cadence twisted her face in confusion. "How?"

"He made me fall for him."

Cadence stood so fast that she knocked the chair over. With a hand to her heart, she gasped, "Oh, Alana!" She picked up her chair and sat back down. "Spill it all, right now," she said.

"That trip was absolutely magical. Well, except for the parts of his race that I saw."

"You weren't there for the entire race?"

"Of course I was." She waved at Cadence as if she'd said something ridiculous.

"What do you mean about the parts you saw?"

"I kept closing my eyes." Alana giggled. "But I did peek through my fingers every now and then. They were moving too fast and those turns—whew! I'm surprised that he didn't leave his kneecap on the track, but he did look incredibly sexy in that biker uniform. I see why the groupies go crazy over them."

Cadence snickered. "Get back to the magical part."

"Cay, he catered to me from the moment I stepped off the airplane until the second we left." Alana shared the details with Cadence, leaving out the truly personal parts. "Beautiful hotels, delicious meals and…those things are great, but what really got me this weekend were the small things. He pays attention to me, Cay—keenly I might add. I never realized how much that mattered. He's arranging for me to meet him in France for his upcoming race. Can you believe that he has a small place out there in the country? This is all happening so fast." Alana put her hand on her head. "He says he wants me to trust him."

"Wow!" Cadence grinned through the entire recap. "So is it official?"

"Yes."

Cadence clapped her hands.

Alana held up a finger and tilted her head. "Don't get happy too fast. We're seeing if this will work out. I don't know how the distance is going to affect us." Alana opened the laptop and hit the power button.

Their assistant, Jennifer, ran into the office, entering like a brisk wind.

"Alana." Jennifer was breathless. "What's the name of that motorcycle racer who came here for you? Is this him?" she asked without giving Alana time to answer. Jennifer shoved her cell phone in front of Alana's face.

Alana had to step back to see the image.

"Let me see." Cadence took the phone. "No. That's not Drew."

"Why?" Alana turned to Cadence. They exchanged confused expressions and looked back at Jennifer.

"Thank goodness. I was reading this article online about a motorcycle racer who was arrested for assault a few weeks back. It's been all over the news, but now he's being sued for a half-million dollars. Someone filmed him being served papers. He lost it. They posted the video on Facebook, and it went viral. There's over a million likes, and the video has only been posted less than a day."

Alana tapped her password into her laptop and typed in the man's name. A full page of headlines, videos and images came up, showing the face of the man he allegedly assaulted. Other pictures depicted the man being cuffed and taken in by the police.

"How did I miss this? I wonder if Drew knows him," Alana said.

"Call him," Cadence prompted.

"He's visiting his dad at the hospital. I don't want to disturb him now."

"You're right. We can ask later."

"He's stopping by later. We were planning a late lunch. I'll ask then." Alana didn't recall seeing Gary Hayden in Austin but assumed that Drew had to know him. She wasn't quite sure how big this motorcycle-racing world was. "In the meantime, we need to get to work. Cadence, did you get a chance to look over the marketing plan I left for you?"

"I did, and I have a few suggestions. How about we start with that and then go to the budget?"

"Sure."

For the next few hours, Cadence and Alana finalized their marketing strategy, hired a PR consultant and held a conference call with their accountant. Then Cadence went back to her office to review briefs.

Alana had completely forgotten to call Drew about her lunch. When she picked up her cell phone, she noticed several missed calls and a few texts. Just as she was about to call him back, Jennifer stuck her head into her office.

"Alana," Jennifer said with a mix of excitement and anxiety, "you won't believe who just came into our office."

Alana's brows furrowed. "Who?"

"That motorcycle guy I showed you this morning. He asked for you and Cadence. Where should I send him?"

Their office was small, consisting of only a reception area and the two offices Alana and Cadence used. Each had a round table that could fit a few chairs, which they often used to spread papers across the room as they worked. Soon enough, they would be able to upgrade to a larger space with an actual conference room.

Alana stood quickly, putting her phone aside. She'd call Drew later.

"Tell him we'll be right with him."

She headed to Cadence's office and closed the door.

"Cay, that biker is here."

Cadence looked confused.

"The one whose video went viral," Alana added.

Cadence's back straightened. "Really?"

"Yep. I'll tell Jen to send him in here."

Cadence started tidying her desk, even though it wasn't really messy. Big clients made you scrutinize your space, so Alana understood her actions. Alana called for Jennifer to bring the client to Cadence's office.

"Gary Hayden," he said, sticking out his hand.

Alana shook it. "Alana Tate. This is my partner."

"Cadence Payne," Cadence interjected as she came around her desk.

"Please have a seat," Alana offered.

"Can we get you anything to drink?" Cadence asked.

"I'm fine, thanks."

The three sat at the table. "What brings you to Payne, Tate and Associates today?"

"It was self-defense." He jumped right in. "He provoked me. Even though I was arrested, the case didn't go anywhere. Then, yesterday, I get these." Gary tossed the papers he had been served on the desk. "He's suing me for half a million dollars."

Cadence and Alana looked at each other.

"Let's start from the beginning," Alana said, guiding him as she and Cadence took notes.

Gary told them that he'd been out celebrating a recent win with fellow bikers in his division when a man began taunting them. The end result was a black eye and one broken rib for the guy and sore knuckles for Gary.

"I need someone who will be able to prove that I'm innocent. I'm sick of these fools trying to chip away at my finances with their false claims. I came here because I heard you're one of the best firms at handling cases where the media loves to create a frenzy."

Alana smiled inside. This was just what their practice needed. They listened to the rest of his story and told him what would be required for representation. Gary didn't hesitate. He pulled out his credit card and handed it to

Cadence. She called Jennifer to process the payment of his retainer and provide Gary with a receipt. The three of them stood and shook hands.

"We're looking forward to working with you, Mr. Hayden. Come on, I'll walk you out," Alana offered.

"The two of you are quite beautiful," Gary added as they left Cadence's office.

"Thanks, but I have to let you know that flattery won't help your case or reduce your fees." Alana raised a brow and chuckled.

"A sense of humor too? If you're as competent as folks say you are, then I'm truly in luck."

Keeping her manner professional, Alana stuck her hand out to shake his. "Mr. Hayden, we'll see you in the morning."

"The pleasure's all mine," Gary said with a frisky grin. "I'm feeling confident about my situation already." His handshake lingered a little too long.

Alana withdrew her hand, placing it behind her back. Nodding, she dismissed him and his flirtatious advance, saying, "Have a great evening."

"What are you doing here?"

Both Alana's and Gary's heads whipped in the direction of Drew's voice, which was coated in insolence and suspicion. Drew glowered at Gary, who glared back at him.

"Hey, Drew. I'll be ready in a moment. You can wait for me in my office, if you'd like." Alana wasn't sure what was happening, but Drew's and Gary's distaste for one another was apparent. She thought it best to immediately defuse anything that could spark a confrontation. There was no need to ask Drew if he knew who Gary was.

Gary looked back and forth between Drew and Alana,

apparently summing up their possible connection. His glare faded, replaced by a smirk.

Drew walked past Gary to where Alana stood, kissed her and posted himself by her side possessively.

Gary turned and walked out, leaving Alana to wonder what had just happened.

Chapter 18

Drew was still standing when Alana returned to her office. The blood coursing through his veins made him too antsy to sit down. Why was Gary there? Was he trying to be slick again?

"What's up with you and this guy, Gary?" Alana asked.

"What was he doing here?" Drew moved closer to Alana.

She stepped back with her hands up. "Whoa! Stand down, cowboy. This is *my* business."

Drew lifted his hands in surrender. "That was out of line. I apologize. I just don't like that guy."

"That wasn't obvious." Alana sat on the edge of her desk and crossed her arms.

Drew chuckled at her sarcasm. Her response prompted him to relax just a little. Alana was certainly capable of taking care of herself. He took a breath and swallowed the rest of his anger before walking over to her. He kissed her and then sat on the desk beside her.

"We're not friends. Seeing him here and so close to you just…reminded me that I don't like him." Drew decided there was no need to go into too much detail. He certainly didn't want to bring up Gary's rendezvous with Jade. Mentioning her name to Alana wouldn't help the situation.

"Wow. That's too bad." She frowned. "He's our new client."

Drew gave her a long, pensive look. "I can't tell you who to do business with, but I would prefer if it wasn't with him."

"Drew!" Alana's mouth was ajar. Drew laughed and kissed her open mouth. "Why don't you want us to work with him? Why don't you two get along?"

"Gary is not a nice guy. In fact, he's a bit of a jerk. Competitive too." Drew paused a moment. "He went after my ex while we were still together."

Alana's posture straightened and her eyes stretched. "Whoa. Okay, I get it now. What's for lunch, mister?" She changed the subject.

"Something tasty," Drew said with mischief in his eyes.

Alana shook her head. She collected her purse and jacket before Drew took her hand and led her to the elevator.

When the door closed, he pulled her into his arms. "I can't get enough of you." He enjoyed making her blush.

Outside, Drew hailed a taxi, giving the driver directions to his destination on the Upper East Side. Drew held Alana's hand throughout the ride and they settled into a companionable silence as the city landscape rolled through the windows.

During lunch, the city unleashed its flood of hungry professionals onto the streets. Business suits walked along with uniformed delivery personnel each looking to outpace the other. No one stood out in this tapestry of colors and cultures except those whose pace resisted the tempo of city living.

Drew loved the rapid rhythm of Manhattan, which energized him. He appreciated the distinct qualities that each of his locales offered. Brooklyn and London both offered equally trendy vibes at a smoother pace. His parents' estate was cozy and inviting, while his chateau in France served as a stunning but tranquil setting where he could completely unwind. Drew wanted Alana to experience all the places he loved.

The taxi pulled up to a building tucked deep into the city's East Side, a few short blocks from the city's typical hustle. He appreciated how solemn the area was even though it was nestled on the rim of one of the busiest parts of New York. Drew paid the taxi, jumped out and reached back to help Alana exit.

"Where are we going?" Alana looked around.

"I need your opinion on something before we eat."

"Okay," Alana elongated the word, eyeing Drew suspiciously. He simply chuckled.

"Mr. Barrington?"

Drew and Alana turned around. A short, hearty woman with a sturdy handshake greeted them both.

"How are you, Mrs. Morano?"

"Oh, please call me Jan. My husband was pretty excited to know that I was showing this place to you today. He's a huge fan of yours."

"That's great. Thanks and feel free to call me Drew. This here is the lovely Alana Tate."

Jan dipped her chin and smiled sweetly. "Pleasure to meet you, Alana. Now let's go check this place out one more time."

Alana looked at Drew again. He acknowledged her inquisitive stare with a clever grin. They followed the woman through the glass doors of the brick building they stood by. A friendly doorman greeted them, holding the elevator open. Jan tapped a few numbers onto the keypad on the elevator panel and a few moments later, the door opened to a spacious apartment with a magnificent view of the Ed Koch Queensboro Bridge reaching across East River.

Drew watched with pleasure as Alana's eyes easily widened. She walked right over to the wall of windows as if the view had summoned her.

"It's absolutely stunning, isn't it?" Jan voiced.

"Completely." Alana scanned the length of the view.

"So here we have a beautiful, open floor plan, which gives a very *lofty* feel," Jan announced with the excitement of a game show host. Her voice bounced around the empty apartment. She held her hands open, gesturing to the spaciousness as she spoke. "As you'll see—" Jan's heels clopped against the hardwood floors "—the kitchen has been completely updated with stainless-steel appliances and amazing slate countertops and floors. You have an abundance of storage space." She opened several of the cabinets lining the two walls. She went on to show them a small library on the opposite side of the dining and living area. "There's a powder room just over there." She pointed to a door just off the kitchen. "Down this way—" Jan led them down the hall "—you'll find two very spacious bedrooms each with a full bath."

Drew took Alana by the hand, leading her through the long hallway.

She looked at Alana and nodded. "Here's one bedroom," Jan offered.

Drew and Alana peeked in. It was an average size. "Not bad." Drew nodded approvingly.

They followed Jan to the second bedroom at the end of the hallway. Jan stopped at the door. "I've saved the best for last." She paused dramatically before swinging the door open. "Your master suite!" She presented the room with a grand, sweeping gesture.

Drew and Alana stepped in. Alana gasped. Drew smiled on the inside. He was impressed with the massive space, closed-in glass balcony overlooking the water and a full wall of closet space. They moved into the master bath with his-and-her sinks, a walk-in shower and horizontally veined marble covering the floor and walls. The bath looked like one that could be found in a luxury hotel.

"Goodness, Drew! This place is incredible. Are you thinking about getting it?"

Jan took that as a sign to leave them alone for a moment.

Drew shrugged. "Maybe. Do you like it?"

"Do I like it?" Alana looked around. "It's incredible. Are you selling your house in Brooklyn?"

"I plan to rent it out and move here. I looked into this because of changes I'd like to make for the future." Drew looked at his watch. "It's time for lunch." He didn't want to reveal too much.

They met Jan in the living room. "Jan—" Drew held his hand out and they shook "—thanks so much. I'll be in touch." Drew held the door for the Jan as she exited the apartment, leaving them behind.

"Great." She smiled at Drew and directed her attention to Alana. "I'm sure you'll help him make the right decision. It was a pleasure meeting you," she said to Alana before saying a final goodbye and stepping onto the elevator.

"Have you decided what you wanted for lunch?" Drew asked Alana once Jan was gone.

"No, but as hungry as I am, anything edible will do." A moment passed. "Drew, are you listening to me?"

"Yes." He quieted again, his hands moving quickly across the screen of his cell phone.

"Hello! I'm still here. That's rude, you know."

Drew laughed. "I'm just taking care of our lunch." Approaching her, he wrapped his hands around her waist. "You're so feisty."

When Alana tried to respond, he hushed her with his lips. They kissed, and time seemed to fade away until they heard the elevator chime and the door slide open. Startled, Alana jumped back.

"Right on time," Drew declared, releasing her.

"What are you up to?"

Drew turned her around to watch the two gentlemen in chef coats wheel in a table covered in white linen with candles and covered plates on top.

Alana's hands flew to her mouth. Her head shook slowly. "You're so full of surprises."

The gentlemen set up the table with a stainless-steel cooler, a bottle of wine nestled in ice and a centerpiece of lilies, Alana's favorite. Drew observed as she reacted in wonder. When the men were sure that met Drew's approval they left as stealthily as they had arrived.

Alana grabbed Drew and hugged him tight. "This is incredible. Why do you keep going to all this trouble to do this crazy stuff?"

"Because I like to see your smile, and you're worth it."

Chapter 19

You're worth it. That comment woke Alana up yet again. No man had ever told her that and backed it up with his actions. She'd been dreaming of their recent excursion and the surprise lunch since that exquisite afternoon. In the past few weeks, Drew had spent more time in the States than he had in years, splitting that time between visiting his father in the rehabilitation center and cuddling with Alana. They couldn't resist one another's touch when they were together and craved each other when they were apart.

Alana and Drew spoke every day, even if it was for just a few moments when the time difference allowed them reasonable intervals. He'd stay up late just to be able to speak to her when she got home after a long day at work.

Alana wouldn't allow Drew to ask too much about her trial with Gary. She had to protect attorney-client privilege, but she also didn't want to upset him. Gary was

Nicki Night   133

proving to be as unlikable as Drew had warned. His arrogance went far beyond reasonable expectations. The media was all over the case, capturing scenes of them entering and leaving the court whenever they could. The trial put their business back in the spotlight and, eventually, they started to pick up more clients.

Despite Gary's obnoxious attitude, business improved. Alana and Cadence had a case to win regardless of how much of an ass their client was. Exhausted by the demands of Gary, the media and new clients, Alana was more than ready to board her flight to France to spend a week with Drew and see his next race. She and Cadence both needed a break and, fortunately, they were able to maneuver their schedules so that business was handled while they took turns enjoying time off.

Drew had Alana picked up and taken to their hotel in Le Mans, France, a culturally robust city that was most famous for their twenty-four-hour car race every June. Spring had taken ahold of the city. Lush parks dotted the town, sharing space with cobbled streets, regal cathedrals, trams, modern shops and slim homes that stood side by side.

Drew had a busy week of participating in media briefs, practicing and qualifying for the race, which is why Alana didn't arrive until the day before. With Alana's full schedule and fifteen-hour flight, including stopovers in both Dublin and Paris, she needed rest as much as Drew did. It wasn't until after his race, which he won, that they really had time to actually commune with one another.

The next morning, Alana accompanied Drew on a photo shoot for Fire Fuel energy drinks, Drew's latest endorsement deal. Watching him pose for picture after picture in his colorful, close-fitting jumpsuit next to a polished silver motorcycle, Alana couldn't wait to get back to the hotel and show Drew how turned on she was.

"Come here, Alana," Drew called her over once the shoot was over.

When Alana got close enough, Drew grabbed her and held tight. The photographer, who had just begun to pack up his materials, took a few shots. Alana threw her head back and laughed, but as she tried to walk away Drew pulled her back and nodded at the photographer. He called his assistant over and they engaged in an impromptu shoot taking sweet photos with them kissing and holding hands, cool photos with their arms folded in hip-hop stances and quirky photos with silly faces. Drew even convinced her to take a few risqué photos with the two of them seated on the motorcycle in various positions. Surprisingly, those made Alana feel sexy and uninhibited.

Drew exchanged numbers with the photographer, who promised to email the pictures to him.

"Are you ready?" Drew asked.

Alana was about ask, *Ready for what?* but held her words, knowing now that Drew wouldn't give her a direct answer. He'd much rather show her.

"I'm ready for whatever."

"You're finally getting it."

Alana attempted to swat him playfully. He caught her hand midair and kissed her palm. Her stomach fluttered, which had happened more in the past few weeks with Drew than she could remember over her entire life. He made energy course through her with just a glance.

"Let's go."

Drew changed and headed to the hotel. The day was still new and Alana was excited for anything Drew would bring her way. They gathered their belongings and checked out. Alana was surprised since she had assumed they would stay there until she left for New York.

Drew arranged for a driver to take them to Paris for sightseeing, shopping, dinner and an evening of live jazz. The next afternoon, they took a long ride through the French countryside, where lush carpets of lavender bloomed in the fields.

As tired as Alana was from their excursions, she refused to go to sleep during their ride and miss the beautiful old villages, colorful homes and cheerful spring blooms lining the canals. She felt like she needed to see everything that Paris had to offer.

Alana looked at Drew quizzically when they pulled up to a lone, quaint home set on an expansive field.

"Are we visiting someone?"

"Nope. Get out of the car, lady."

Alana rolled her eyes. "You're too much, Drew."

"I know. You'll never be able to compare me to another man."

"And so darn arrogant."

Drew responded with a sly smile. "It's not arrogance when it's true, sweetie. Now let's get inside. This air is a little nippy."

Alana looked around trying to see what she could through the blackness of the night. The only light came from the car's headlights. She followed Drew inside. He flipped on the lights and she looked around, immediately feeling the warmth of the cozy setting. In spite of being thousands of miles away, she felt like she was at her grandmother's country home in North Carolina.

"Whose place is this?" she asked, inspecting the comfortable two-story home while Drew placed their bags in the living room. The place was decorated in soft, inviting earth tones. Alana wondered what woman had put her touch on the house.

"Mine." The word fell casually from Drew's lips but hit Alana like a boulder.

This man was truly full of surprises. "Do I even know you?" she teased.

Drew turned and headed back to the kitchen, leaving Alana to ponder what she had learned about him in the past few weeks. She realized she'd only known a part of Drew's life.

"Actually, you know me better than anyone." He walked to the kitchen and pulled a bottle of wine from a cooler. "Wine or tea?" He continued moving about, seemingly oblivious to her amazement.

"I've known you for years and never realized you lived like this."

"I also own a flat in London, and I just signed the papers on the place you approved of on the East Side." Drew spoke as if owning amazing homes all over the world was commonplace.

"You bought that place?"

"Yeah, I've always wanted to live in Manhattan." He held up a bottle of wine in one hand and a teakettle in the other.

"Wine, thanks."

He headed back to the kitchen as he continued to speak. "Each place gives me something different, but this place just might be my favorite. I do most of my reflecting here. Right outside of this door—" Drew pointed toward the door at the back of the kitchen with his elbow, his hands holding two glasses of wine "—is where some of my biggest ideas manifest. It's peaceful here."

"Wow." Alana thought back to the day Drew took her and Cadence to that restaurant for lunch and he spoke

French to the hostess. "So this is where you learned how to flirt so fluidly in French."

Drew winked as he set the glasses down on a coffee table and sat on the couch, patting the space beside him. "Join me." She did.

Alana clinked her glass against his. "Cheers." She took a sip and lolled her head back. "My goodness. This is so good."

"It's from a winery a few miles down the road."

"This is the life. I'd never leave here."

"Not until you get a craving for the city." He lifted himself up. "Come on, let me show you the back."

Alana picked up her glass and followed him out to a closed-in porch, complete with more cozy couches, a TV, a sparsely stocked bar, hot tub and one of his motorcycles. Alana wondered how many women he had entertained in that hot tub.

"Entertain much?" she asked, cutting back more probing questions.

"I know what you're thinking and, to answer your real question, the only woman who has ever been in that tub was my ex-girlfriend."

"Jade," Alana said almost at a whisper.

Alana went over to his bike.

"That's Jolie," he said leaning against the door frame.

"You named the motorcycle?" she asked, wrapping her fingers around one of the handlebars.

"I name all of them."

The bike was beautiful in an edgy way and stood firmly in a stand as if it were a featured exhibit in a museum. Alana ran her fingers along the seat.

"Don't do that," Drew said.

"Don't do what?" Alana was confused. She continued running her hands along the body of the bike.

"That."

Alana realized he was talking about the motorcycle. "You mean this?" Alana leaned forward and pressed her body against the bike, sliding her hands across it seductively.

"Yes. That." The tone of Drew's voice sank and became husky.

Alana teased him, stroking the motorcycle as tenderly as she would a lover. Drew looked like he held back a smile, but the desire in his expression was clear. Alana giggled, enjoying the effect that handling the bike in such a way had on Drew.

Putting down his glass, Drew stood and slowly sauntered over to where Alana put on her show with his motorcycle. He caressed her back, which arched instinctively from his touch. Immediately, heat spread throughout her body, causing her skin to tingle.

Drew straddled the bike, guiding her on to face him. She leaned back toward the handles, her breath guiding her chest up and down in a syncopated rhythm. Drew leaned toward her, sliding his tongue into her warm mouth. The sounds of their kiss echoed. Drew pulled Alana's shirt up, skillfully unsnapped her bra in a single motion and released her mounds. As he took her nipples between his teeth, they pebbled. Alana leaned forward. Grabbing him, she held on and kissed him back, hard. Moans rumbled in their throats.

Taking the lead, Alana pulled Drew's shirt over his head, tossed it and fondled his taut chest. Drew hissed when she took his nipples into her mouth. He removed her shirt and they held each other, bare chest to bare chest as desire bubbled between them. She ground herself against his firm erection.

Drew dismounted the bike, took Alana by the hand

and helped her off too. Carefully, he peeled off the rest of her clothes and then his. They stared at each other for a moment. Alana felt something shift inside of her. All the effort placed into blocking Drew from penetrating her heart had failed. Alana stood before him, staring into his soul, wanting to connect with him in a cavernous way that she'd never desired before. His body was art, a joy for the eye to feast on, but her appreciation for the man inside that glorious casing had increased exponentially.

Drew snaked his hand around her lower back and brought her closer. Another kiss. He rested her hands on the seat of the bike and explored her body right where she stood. Burying his head between her spread thighs, he lapped until her legs became too unstable to stand on. Leading her toward the front of the bike, he placed her hands on the handlebars, bent her forward and sheathed himself.

Drew planted a trail of kisses down her back. Alana's center tightened in anticipation of him. She wanted to feel him already. He entered slow and deep. Alana sucked in air. Drew hissed. Together they found a delicious rhythm, luxuriated in it until her heart beat in her ear like drums. Drew's grunts let her know that he was reaching a breaking point. Alana tightened her walls around him snuggly and squeezed him. Drew jerked. Their tempo increased urgently. Alana chanted his name and he exploded, collapsing onto her back.

Drew caught his breath. "Alana," he whispered in her ear from behind.

"Yes," she replied breathlessly.

"I'm gonna make you love me."

Chapter 20

"You boys have to play that music so loud?" Joyce yelled over Drew's party playlist. Though she hollered at her sons, she looked at Alana, Cadence and Chey and threw her hands up as if she was exasperated, but everyone knew how much Joyce loved having her family around.

The Barrington estate hummed with the pleasant sounds of a family gathering. Chatter, laughter and music blended together to create a merry symphony. Floyd was proudly perched at the head of the table for the first time in months.

"Aw, Joycie, let the boys have their fun." Floyd spoke slowly, still managing a slightly lazy tongue, one of the remaining side effects from his stroke.

Joyce peered at Floyd over her glass and then opened a large pot to stir the green beans.

"Hey, woman! Get back!" Drew took the spoon from her hand. "You're supposed to be sitting down. We've got this."

"Exactly. We've got this," Blake echoed. "Why make us learn how to cook if you're never going to let us do it?"

"Alright, I'm sitting." Joyce parked herself next to Floyd and patted his hand.

Drew and Blake continued preparing Sunday dinner as they waited for Hunter to get back from the store with more eggs. Alana, Cadence and Chey sat around the table chatting with Joyce and Floyd since they weren't allowed to help cook.

Hunter blew into the kitchen like a violent wind. "I got the eggs."

Blake took a few bags from him.

"Give me two eggs for the mac and cheese so I can put it in the oven," Drew said.

Hunter handed him the eggs, and Drew danced back to the cabinet to retrieve a bowl to beat them in. Drew danced through every step of his meal preparation, matching his movements to the tempo.

"Leave room in the oven for my cornbread," Hunter instructed.

"Can you believe this, Floyd?" Joyce yelled.

Drew turned down the music just a bit so his mother wouldn't have to keep yelling.

"Thank you!" Joyce threw both hands up in the air as if lowering music was a gift from God.

"Okay, now taste this." Drew scooped a small forkful of his herb jasmine rice and fed it to Joyce.

"Yum! I taught you well, didn't I?"

"Uh, Ma, you didn't teach me that." Drew said and ducked his mother's playful whack just in time. Everyone laughed.

"Boy, I taught you how to cook and that's all that matters."

"I still cook better than both of you," Hunter interjected.

"What?" Drew and Blake said simultaneously.

"Blake, do you remember that day Hunter burned those boiled eggs? We came into the kitchen and they were no longer in the pot." Drew doubled over laughing.

Blake cackled until he could hardly catch his breath. "And then we finally looked up and saw they were stuck to the ceiling."

"No! Hunter, say it isn't so!" Chey's entire upper body rocked as she laughed.

"That's your man, Chey." Drew pointed at her with the spoon he used to stir the green beans. "Burning boiled eggs. Who does that?"

"Oh yeah? Well, what about that fire you started when you were trying to fry chicken that night when we were at your house watching the Super Bowl."

"Oh—" Floyd lifted a wobbly finger "—I remember that!" He chuckled slow and easy.

"Floyd! You never told me about that." Joyce looked genuinely surprised.

"Blake, what about that chicken you messed up at your BBQ that time?" Hunter said.

"That doesn't count. I was hungover."

"So was I when I set the kitchen on fire," Drew said, exaggerating. "Those times shouldn't count. What was your excuse, Hunter? You weren't hungover when those eggs went airborne."

The brothers kept the family entertained with their joshing and stories of capers as they finished dinner. The women helped them set the table.

Joyce said a moving grace, thanking God for bringing her husband home and her family together. She ended by saying, "Lord, if you see to it that I get some grandkids I'll be forever grateful."

Drew's eyes popped open and he noticed that Blake's and Hunter's had done the same. They snickered without making a sound. He looked over at Alana. Her head was still down and her eyes closed. As much as he joked, he looked forward to one day having a family with her. He had meant it when he told her that he planned to make her love him. Drew wasn't sure if he could call what he felt for her love just yet, but he knew it was close to it.

"Amen," Joyce finally said and everyone sat down.

"Pass me a piece of Hunter's cornbread. Let me see if it's better than mine," Drew teased. They continued the banter until someone rang the bell, surprising them all into silence.

"You're expecting company, Ma?" Hunter asked as he headed to the door.

"No." Joyce looked as surprised as her husband and sons.

Hunter walked back into the room with an unreadable expression.

"Who is it, baby?" Joyce asked.

"Hi, everyone!" Jade stepped from behind Hunter. "It's been such a long time."

Several moments dragged by before anyone spoke. Blake looked at Drew. Drew looked at Alana.

"Hi, honey." Joyce stood and approached Jade, rescuing them all from the awkward silence. "We just sat down for dinner."

"Hey, Jade. Long time no see." Blake finally spoke. The others followed his lead.

Drew wasn't uncomfortable. He just wanted to know why Jade had to choose today, of all days, to stop by his parents' house.

"What brings you by, dear?" Joyce asked, still standing between Jade and the table. Drew understood his mother's actions. She was making sure Jade kept a considerable distance in the presence of Alana.

"Yes, Jade, what brings you by?" Drew asked. "Oh, please pardon my manners," he added before she could answer. "This is Blake's fiancée, Cadence, Hunter's fiancée, Chey, and my girlfriend, Alana."

Nice-to-meet-yous were politely exchanged. Jade's eye lingered on Alana and, suddenly, she looked uncomfortable.

"I was in the area and heard about Mr. Barrington. When I rode by, I saw all the cars and figured it would be a good time to catch someone at home. You look well, Mr. B. I hope you're feeling good."

"I'm getting there. One day at a time. Thanks for stopping by."

Another few moments of awkward silence settled in until Joyce asked Jade if she wanted something to eat.

"Sure, I'd love to stick around for a moment and catch up."

Drew sighed inwardly, but he understood his mother's hospitality wouldn't allow her to be rude. She would have offered a plate to anyone who knocked on that door.

"Hunter, darling, could you fix Jade a plate?" Joyce said with a tight smile. "Come on over here and sit right by me, sweetheart. Blake, sweetie, get that chair over there and bring it next to me."

Hunter and Blake did as they were told. As they continued their meal in the presence of their unexpected guest, the easy banter of their earlier conversation dissipated, replaced by strained small talk. Joyce worked to keep the conversation on neutral ground, but Jade kept directing it back to Drew.

"Congratulations on your recent win."

Instinctively, Drew craned his neck and massaged his shoulder. "Thanks." He hadn't mentioned anything to Alana or his brothers, but his shoulder still got pretty sore at times and the tension of having Jade and Alana at the same table caused some of the soreness to emerge now. It could have been in his mind, but he was pretty sure that Jade's visit had brought it on.

"What's new with you?" she asked.

Everyone at the table looked back and forth from Jade to Drew as if they were watching a ping-pong match.

"Not much. I'm starting to think about what I'd like to do after I'm done with racing."

"You're quitting?"

"Not just yet. Just thinking about my next move, that's all. When I'm ready to make that shift, I want it to be a smooth transition. I'd love to possibly do some broadcasting or something like that."

"Oh, I could help you with that. My family's company represents quite a few folks in broadcasting. We've recently expanded and can help you with publicity, personal brand management and all kinds of opportunities. Actually, our company is quite influential in the industry."

"That's cool. Maybe we can chat about that," Drew said in a noncommittal way.

"Sure. That would be great."

Drew didn't miss the quick glance Alana gave him. "I'm not looking to do anything just yet."

"What's the name of your family's company?" Cadence asked.

"The Donnelly Group. Our client list is pretty impressive."

"Anyone we would know?" Chey inquired.

Drew wondered how authentic their questions were, knowing that they would undoubtedly have Alana's back.

"Of course." Jade rattled off a few well-known celebrities, broadcasters and athletes. "We've helped several athletes transition into lucrative opportunities in the spotlight. We brokered the deal to get David Stanton his spot on the morning show on channel seven when he retired from basketball."

"Oh, really?" Cadence said.

"Yes. We could help you do something like that too, Drew. The camera has always loved a pretty face."

The room went silent once again.

Seeming oblivious to the tension she carried in with her, Jade stayed for another hour, sticking around for Blake's rich, moist chocolate pound cake, Hunter's delicious sweet potato pie and Drew's decadent chocolate croissants.

"I'm stuffed. Everything was so good. You always were a great cook, Mrs. Barrington."

"Thanks. I'd love to take the credit, but my sons did all of the cooking today," Joyce explained.

Jade's gasp was dramatic. "Really? Well I'm sure they learned it all from you."

"Of course they did." Joyce gave her a quick smile. "Have a good night and thanks for stopping by, dear."

"You're welcome." Jade embraced Joyce. "Glad to see you're doing well, Mr. Barrington. My dad will be happy to hear that. Good night, everyone." They all offered polite goodbyes. She started for the door and paused. "Um. Drew, may I speak to you for a moment?"

He didn't answer right away. Instead he passed Alana a subtle look and she raised her brow just as subtly, giving him an unspoken green light. He also noticed the looks on everyone's faces as they awaited his response.

"Sure," Drew finally said. "I'll walk you out."

"She seems nice," Jade said once they made it to the door and were out of earshot.

"She is." Drew's smile was genuine. It happened involuntarily every time he thought of Alana.

"That's great." She looked down at her hands. "Here's my card. I could really help you with your transition. Give me a call."

Reluctantly, Drew took the card. "Thanks." He looked back.

"It was nice seeing you again, Drew. I'm glad we're able to…put the past behind us."

"Yeah." Drew looked back toward the dining kitchen again.

Neither of them spoke for a few moments.

"I need to get going." She smiled but didn't move.

"Nice of you to stop by. I'm sure my dad appreciates it. Get home safe." Drew opened the door, but Jade stayed put for another moment before walking out unhurriedly. "Good night."

Drew hadn't told anyone, but there was a chance that his transition could happen sooner than he had planned. This was his second dislocation in the past year. His doctor had warned him after his last injury that he needed to seriously consider retiring because his shoulder wasn't healing the way they had anticipated. Drew felt the difference after every race. He had worked hard to win that last one, attentively nursing his shoulder before Alana arrived.

He loved racing and, if he was going to be forced to retire, Drew was determined to go out with a big win. This season meant everything to him. He would certainly need the services of The Donnelly Group, but he didn't know if he should do business with Jade. However, if he could handle Alana working with Gary, then maybe, just maybe, it would be okay to work with Jade. He would just have to make sure Jade knew where he stood.

Chapter 21

The ride home with Drew after dinner had Alana on edge. Drew spent the night just as he did most nights when he was in the States, but this night was different. It was void of their usual, electrifying, sensual chemistry. They simply cuddled and fell asleep when she claimed to be too tired for sex. Still Drew held her as if she was all that mattered in the world.

The next morning, Alana chided herself for even letting Jade's presence get to her, but she couldn't help being reminded of the sting she felt when Jade had returned to town to reclaim Drew years ago. Alana and Drew hadn't been dating long at the time, but she felt that they'd had potential. It didn't take much for Jade to take him back, which left Alana on the sidelines.

Alana's womanly instincts told her that Jade wanted more than just to pop in for old times' sake. She wanted Drew back—once again. What if Drew was willing to give her another shot? Where would that leave Alana? She couldn't subject herself to that situation again. Jade's visit prompted Alana to begin reconstructing the barriers around her heart. Alana was tired, not from lack of sleep but from overthinking the Jade situation all night.

Drew leaned against the frame of the bathroom door as she painted her lips with a creamy pink matte.

"Good morning." His voice was extra deep whenever he first woke up. That had always turned Alana on. Right now, she was too preoccupied with her thoughts to appreciate that or the fact that he stood there in all his natural glory as if he was fully dressed. "Feeling any better this morning?" he asked.

"I'm fine." She didn't intend her answer to sound so short, but what else could she say? She wasn't going to admit how much Jade's presence rattled her. Despite what intuition told her, she was curious to see how Drew would handle Jade's return.

Alana was used to seeing woman pine after him—especially once she started attending his races. However, those women didn't have the history that he and Jade shared. None of them seemed threatening. Alana thought about his home in the French countryside. Jade had been the only other woman he'd brought there—so he said.

"Alana."

"Huh?"

"I asked if you wanted me to make you a cup of coffee."

"Oh. Sure." Her thoughts had drowned him out.

Alana huffed when she knew Drew had reached downstairs. She hated to be so affected. Drew had introduced her as his girlfriend. Although they'd been dating exclusively for a few months now, they had never put a label on what was happening between them.

Alana finished dressing for work, grabbed her purse and headed downstairs. The nutty aroma of her favorite hazelnut coffee met her halfway down. Drew had placed two boiled eggs and a slice of wheat toast on the table with a cup of coffee and a glass of orange juice. His proclivity to take care of every need had become natural. That made her feel extra special—a feeling that had been absent during her previous relationships.

Alana sat at the table. Drew joined her with a napkin and his own cup of coffee.

"So, I'm your girlfriend, now?" She tried to spark their usual banter to restore their sense of normalcy.

"Did that surprise you?"

"Not really. It's just that we never really put a label on what we were doing here. It was just interesting to hear."

"I know. It *was* interesting to hear, even though I'm the one who said it." Drew sipped his coffee. "It's the only label that makes sense now. I've honestly never been this way with any other woman."

She wanted to ask about Jade but kept the words behind her lips. "Really?" she asked instead. "Then why me?" She bit into her toast.

"Want to know the truth?"

Alana put her fork down. "Yes."

"Well—" Drew paused, making Alana squirm in anticipation "—I just feel like it is supposed to be you." Her breath caught. Drew continued. "I knew I had to reshape your perspective of me. I wasn't serious back when we first started dating and I made some bad decisions. Also, I understood that you had been hurt recently and I wanted to show you that your heart was safe with me. I don't mind putting in the effort. I enjoy trying to impress you and making you smile."

Alana couldn't help but blush. Now, she felt bad for snubbing him last night. "That was sweet."

"That was the truth." Drew's eyes penetrated hers with so much intensity she had to look away.

"What time does your flight leave tonight?" she asked.

"9:25 p.m."

"What time will you get into Florence?"

"It will be around seven thirty in the morning here, but around twelve thirty there."

"Good. Then you'll have time to rest before the media briefs, practice and all of that stuff."

"Yeah." Drew kept looking right into Alana's eyes as he spoke.

"I've never been to Italy." She sat back, avoiding the scrutiny. She felt like he could read her. Alana continued her breakfast even though her appetite was nonexistent.

"We'll have to arrange a trip sometime soon, when you can get more time. How's the case going?"

Drew had stopped using Gary's name when he asked about the case.

"Not much has happened. He's still a jerk. He refuses to settle and if it goes to trial, we're going to have to really work on his image. The courts love making examples out of arrogant rich people. If he doesn't curb his attitude, it could hurt the case. It really does appear that he was provoked by someone looking for a payday."

Drew didn't say much in response.

"Why don't you like him?" she asked.

Drew sighed. He poured some juice and drained the glass. "Things really went awry when he made several advances toward Jade while we were dating. Actually, they ended up having an affair—that's part of the reason Jade and I broke up. They stayed together for a while after our breakup. Eventually she found out he was a jerk too. From what I recall, they didn't last very long."

"Oh!" Alana's eyes grew wide. "I completely understand now."

"That's all behind me, but he's still a jerk. That's why I hate the fact that you're working with him. I'm thinking about taking Jade up on her offer to use the services of her family's business."

Alana sat back in her chair hard. "Is that why you asked about Gary? So it could give you leverage when you told me about working with Jade?"

"No, I always ask you about work. I think I can learn a lot from her about this process—especially now that I'm much more serious about transitioning out of racing. Her family's company is the best in the business."

Suddenly Alana wasn't so hungry anymore. "Hey—" she surrendered her hands in the air "—we shouldn't mix business with the personal. It wouldn't be fair for you to tell me which clients I can represent. I can't dictate whom you should hire to manage your brand. If she can get the job done, work with her." Alana left the kitchen, hoping her true feelings didn't show. The last thing she wanted was to see Jade and Drew in close proximity again. She was professional and professionals hired those people they felt could do the job. She just wished it wasn't Jade.

Her train to work wasn't coming for another forty minutes and the station was only five minutes away, but she needed to get out of house. Alana retrieved a jacket from the closet and picked up her keys.

"Have a safe flight. Call me when you land." She tried to sound like her ususal cheerful self. She couldn't hand her heart over to Drew just for him and his ex to trample all over it.

"Alana."

She turned. Drew touched her arm just as she was about to walk through the front door. He searched her eyes for a moment. She swallowed and looked away.

"Please don't get upset? There's nothing going on with Jade and me. I'm not interested in her like that."

"Anymore…" Alana sighed. "I shouldn't have said that." She'd let her attitude get the best of her and hated that it made her respond in such a childish way but couldn't help but remember that it was Jade who had moved her out of the way years ago and Drew went running back to her.

"I made that mistake a long time ago. I have you now. A lot has changed since then."

"I know." She shifted her weight to one leg. "Dealing with exes can be a challenge."

"I know, but not in this case." Drew cupped her face in his hands. "You're *ma belle.*" He kissed her lips.

Alana huffed then forced a smile. "I'm not crazy about this, but it is business. I get it."

"And you know where I stand with you," Drew added.

Alana remained quiet.

"You can trust me." Drew said.

How can I be sure? Alana sighed, gave him a quick kiss on the lips and headed through the door.

Drew called her one more time. She stopped, turned and gave him a weak smile that she didn't feel in her heart.

Work swallowed up most of Alana's focus and time, leaving little opportunity to mull over Drew's decision to work with Jade. He'd called several times throughout the morning. When she finally answered she kept the conversation brief and used the excuse of being very busy.

By that afternoon, she missed talking to him as much as she usually did.

Alana couldn't knowingly set herself up for more heartbreak. She wanted to believe Drew was sincere. Her mind wrestled with her heart. She remembered how he made her stomach flutter when he said that he felt like she was supposed to be the one and spoke of how much he enjoyed making her smile. Then she thought about Jade and returning to her vow of leaving dating alone for a while. Alana returned her focus to work, a welcome distraction.

The brief she had in her hand made no sense. She'd been reading it for a half hour but had absorbed none of what she read. Finally, she realized it was one of the cases that Cadence had been handling when they split the workload. She headed to Cadence's office to hand it over.

"Maybe you should go home," Cadence said the second Alana's foot hit her door frame.

"Why?" Alana flopped into the chair in front of Cadence's desk.

"Because you look like you didn't get any sleep."

"I didn't." After a deep breath, Alana rolled her head back and slumped in the chair.

"Does it have anything to do with the dinner yesterday?"

"I can't lie. Yes, it does. And there's more."

"I couldn't believe she showed up like that," Cadence said.

"I can't believe he's considering taking her up on her offer to help him with publicity."

"What?" Cadence knocked her cup over. Fortunately it was empty. "What did you say?"

"What can I say? If he had his way, we wouldn't be representing Gary. This is business, Cay. I can't dictate who he should work with, just like he can't dictate who I represent as an attorney. Drew claims her family's company is the best in the business. Who wouldn't want the best?"

"You've got a point, but there's got to be something that can be done. I'll have Blake talk to him."

"No, Cadence. I don't want to make a big deal out of it. Besides, he just said he was thinking about it. Nothing has been solidified."

Cadence grunted. "Why did she have to show up? I wonder if there's more to the visit than just checking in on Mr. Barrington."

"My gut tells me yes."

"Mine too."

The two sat quietly for a moment, pondering the situation. Cadence stared at Alana.

"What?"

"You're not going to break up with him because of this, are you?"

Alana turned away.

"Alana."

"I don't know. I've been here before, Cay. I don't want to get hurt."

"You really believe that the same thing will happen?" Cadence sucked her teeth.

Alana stood and put the brief on Cadence's desk. "I came in here to give this to you." She turned to walk out. Cadence came around her desk and blocked the door.

"No. Don't walk out of my office like this." She closed the door, folded her arms and tapped her foot. "You wouldn't let me walk out like that and I'm not going to let you do it."

Alana sucked in a long breath and shook her head.

"Have a seat and let's talk about this." Cadence pointed

toward the chair and waited for Alana to sit before continuing. "I know how you feel. You know I do because I've been where you are and you helped me through." Cadence sat. "You've never been one to give up so easily, so why now? Drew has gone out of his way to prove to you that he truly cares."

Alana looked down at her fingers. Cadence was right, but she couldn't risk having her heart crushed again. "What if Jade wants Drew back? What if he wants her? I can't go through this again. It's too much."

"Even his brothers are surprised. Drew hasn't had a girl over for a family gathering in years. Don't be unreasonable. He even asked for my help."

That got Alana's attention. "Asked for your help for what?"

"To find out what he needed to do to show you that he was serious. I told him to pay attention. A woman loves it when men pay attention. And I know for sure that he's done a very good job of doing that. If you walk away prematurely, you could miss out on the best relationship you've ever had. Drew has done so much to prove himself. He deserves a little trust."

Alana twisted her lips. That was all she could do, since she couldn't deny that Cadence was telling the truth. It was easy for her to see the bright side since her heart wasn't on the proverbial chopping block. This only made her feel more conflicted.

"Pick up the phone and talk to the man when he calls. He's worried about you."

"How would you know?" Alana asked, but she already knew the answer. She'd ignored most of Drew's calls since she arrived at work.

Cadence just smiled. She didn't have to admit that

Drew called her. The smirk on Cadence's face revealed all Alana needed to know.

Alana promised to think about what her best friend said, but if she moved forward with Drew and their relationship went awry, she would be devastated. Alana wasn't sure if she was willing to gamble that hard. Walking away now would hurt so much less than losing Drew to Jade a second time.

Chapter 22

Drew arrived in Florence around noon local time. The first thing he did was call Alana to let her know he'd arrived. He crashed when he'd finally filled his stomach at his favorite restaurant. Josephina's was a quaint mom-and-pop shop on a cobbled street, where he was treated like family despite his limited linguistic abilities. After he downed a healthy helping of freshly made pasta and two glasses of Limoncello, jet lag ushered him into a sleep that felt like it lasted for days.

Drew's eyes popped open when he heard the phone ring. Disoriented, he adjusted his eyes to the darkness and looked at the clock. It was past midnight. The phone had stopped ringing by the time he reached for it. Drew swung his legs over the side of the bed and rubbed his eyes. Wading through the dark, he made it to the bathroom and remembered he was in Italy. Back in the bedroom, he checked his cell phone for the date and time. The haze was clearing.

Now that he was much more coherent, he swiped his cell to dial Alana's number, but Jade's call came through first.

"Hello."

"Hey there. I'm calling so we can talk about what you'd like to do. I put something together that I think you'll like."

"Jade?"

"Of course. Don't tell me you've forgotten what I sound like on the phone."

"No, I just woke up."

"Woke up? It's just after seven."

"I'm overseas. It's after midnight here."

"Oh, I'm sorry to wake you."

"It's no problem. Tell me about what you put together."

"Yes, okay." Jade's excitement was evident. She went on to propose two paths that he could take for life beyond the track, which included broadcasting. She'd already reached out to a few contacts who would love to meet with him.

"That sounds amazing." Her plans excited Drew. He could see the possibilities.

Jade explained that they worked with both companies and individuals to help them establish, shape, recreate and manage their professional brands, as well as doing PR work and providing other services. "Since I joined the company a few years ago, we've been very successful helping a few of our clients navigate some very dynamic career shifts. I could easily see you in television, whether you go into sports as a broadcaster or TV personality or as a spokesperson or something else along those lines. I can email you what I proposed and when you get back to the States, we can meet and discuss it in further detail."

"That sounds great."

"When will you be home?"

"Next Tuesday."

"Okay, let me check my calendar." Jade quieted for a moment. "How about we do dinner that Wednesday? We can review the proposal. I can answer any questions you have and then we can catch up."

"Yeah, sure." Drew was all for reviewing the proposal but not that interested in the catching-up part. "How about we meet at your office?"

"My schedule is booked. Wednesday evening is the only day I'm free and I'd love to get started on this ASAP."

Drew hesitated a moment. "Okay. Let's do it."

"Great. It's in my calendar. How's the racing world treating you? I see you've changed teams."

"Yes. How'd you know?"

"I check you out every now and then."

Drew wondered why since she was the one who left him for a person he couldn't stand.

"That's interesting and a little unexpected."

"How so?"

"It doesn't really matter."

"You haven't thought about me since we broke up?" Jade sounded disappointed.

Drew got up from the bed. This conversation was going in a direction that he wasn't interested in heading toward. He slipped on a pair of lounge pants and adjusted the room temperature. "At times, when I'm reminded of some things."

"Like what?"

"Like the reason for the breakup."

"Oh." She didn't have much to say. A few beats thumped by. "I'd love to get past that."

"We did. It's now in the past." Drew heard Jade clear

her throat. He'd reached the kitchen of his hotel suite and searched the mini fridge for a bottle of water.

"Do you still have that little chateau in France?"

"Yes, I do. In fact, Alana and I spent some time there a few weeks ago. You remember my girlfriend, Alana. She was at my parents' house when you stopped by on Sunday." Drew knew Jade didn't need reminding. Jade knew who Alana was when she came back to reclaim him years ago. He still regretted falling for Jade a second time.

After a while, she finally responded. "Yes. She's pretty." Jade giggled. "I think it's interesting that you actually went back to her."

"Thanks. I think so too."

"Been together long?" Jade sounded hesitant. Drew wondered if she was sizing up what she thought was competition.

"We recently got back together."

"Interesting."

"What makes you say that?"

"Our situation."

Drew pulled the phone away from his face, looked at it and placed it back to his ear. *Was that a dig?* "If you could email me the proposal by Sunday night, that would be great." Drew didn't want to play this game with Jade.

"I can send it tonight. Call me if you need me to explain anything."

"Okay, I need to get back to sleep. Media briefs are tomorrow and it's pretty late here."

"No problem. Go right ahead. See you next Wednesday?"

"Yep."

"Take care, Drew."

Drew ended the call and immediately dialed Alana.

She didn't answer. With his feet up on the couch, he checked in with his brothers and parents, spending several moments on the phone with each. After that, he dialed Alana again.

"Hey."

"Miss me yet?"

"I will admit that I miss you."

"I can't tell when you don't answer my calls. I'm a long way from home. I don't like feeling like we're estranged."

"We're not estranged, Drew."

"It feels like we are." He waited for her to deny that. She didn't. "Jade is not a threat."

"I didn't say anything about Jade."

"You didn't have to."

Alana quieted again.

"I care about you and only you. You have absolutely nothing to worry about, alright?" Drew imagined her with her eyes closed, counting breaths. "You know you're *ma belle*. No one can take your place."

"I know, Drew." After a few moments, Alana asked, "Isn't it late there?"

"Around one in the morning." Drew headed back to the bedroom of his suite.

"You should go to bed. Call me when you wake up."

"Dream about me," Drew said. He heard Alana chuckle and envisioned her smile. "Good night."

"Good night."

Drew knew that Alana wasn't convinced about Jade not being a threat. Soon enough she would see for herself. He'd prove that to her, as well.

Chapter 23

Judge Ledger banged her gavel and ordered Gary to stop yelling, threatening to hold him in contempt if he walked out her courtroom. Ignoring her, he shoved the doors open and walked right through, flipping his hand over his head and dismissing her demands. Exasperated, Alana told Cadence to stay put while she ran after him.

"Gary!" she screamed once she cleared the courtroom doors.

"What?" He stopped and turned around but then continued walking.

Alana trekked as fast and as carefully as she could on her three-inch pumps.

"What the hell was that?" she said when she caught up with him. Alana looked around at the few people whose attention they had garnered. "Come here." She grabbed his arm and led him farther down the hall to a bench. Too wound up to sit, she checked her surroundings to ensure that she had a little more privacy. "Are you crazy?"

"Who does that judge think she is telling me I need to work out a settlement? I hit him after he hit me. He's a liar who just wants my money."

"She's the judge, that's who. And if she decides that you need to pay, that's exactly what you'll have to do!" With one hand on her hip and one hand on her forehead, Alana looked around again and then lowered her voice. "We have warned you about your attitude. Calm yourself down and get back in that courtroom. Hopefully she won't throw you in jail for contempt." She turned to go to the courtroom, paused and got back in his face. Her finger was inches from his nose. "If this goes wrong, it will be your fault. You hired us to represent you—now let us do our jobs. Otherwise, you can find another firm."

Gary's nose flared. "Don't threaten me. I could always find someone else to represent me."

"Then do it." Alana was done. She marched down the hall and through the doors. Drew had warned her that Gary was a jerk. That was clear to her now.

"Counselor, where is that client of yours?" the judge barked as soon as she entered.

"Your Honor, please excuse his behavior. I'm not sure if he will return, and I'm also not sure if we will continue to represent him." Alana was out of breath.

Cadence eye's bulged at Alana's comment. *What?* she mouthed with her face twisted in confusion.

"I'm right here, Your Honor."

"Bailiff, take him in. I'm holding you in contempt. One wrong move and this will be your home for the next thirty days. Do you hear me?"

Alana and Cadence sighed simultaneously.

Judge Ledger banged her gavel. "I'll see the rest of you on the third of next month. Make sure you teach your client how to act in my courtroom." She pointed her gavel in Alana and Cadence's direction.

"Yes, Your Honor," they said together.

Alana slammed her folder shut and stuffed it in her briefcase. She could tell by Cadence's tight lip that she was just as angry. When she looked over at the plaintiff, he sported a smirk and she wanted to snatch it off his face. They briefly visited with Gary before heading straight back to their office.

"I can't believe this." Alana paced the small space inside Cadence's office.

"Me either." Cadence flopped into her chair.

"I wanted to pop him in the mouth," Alana said.

"What about when he said, 'Now I know you're more than just two pretty faces'?" Cadence lowered her voice, mocking him. "And after all of that he still wants us to represent him."

"I can't wait until this trial is over." Alana groaned.

"I know. We need to figure out how we can salvage this case and get a win. I'll scour the police reports again for anything that might stand out."

"Did the police ever get back to us about the cameras in the area?" Alana wondered aloud.

"Hmm. Not sure."

"I'll check into that," Alana offered.

For the next hour, as they ate lunch, they deliberated over Gary's recent antics and other strategies to win this case. Alana then retreated to her office to work on other cases. Five o'clock came sooner than they realized. She looked at her phone and noticed she'd missed several calls, including two from Drew. She sighed.

Alana had spoken to Drew much less frequently in the past few days. He'd asked if she would join him and Jade for their dinner meeting tonight. He wanted to get her opinion. Fortunately she had a real commitment which caused her to have to decline his offer. She couldn't picture herself sharing a table with Drew and his ex. That commitment reminded her to make sure that Cadence would be joining her at the NYAA meeting.

"Cadence," Alana called as she walked the few steps to her office. She stuck her head just past the door frame. "You're coming with me tonight, right?"

"Yes."

"Good. I was just confirming." Alana had finally convinced Cadence to join the New York Association of Attorneys, arguing that it would be good for their firm. She wasn't as active as Alana was, but she attended meetings on a regular basis. Alana was fine with that. "Okay. Let's head over at six."

When Alana got back to her office, her cell phone buzzed. It was Drew again. She sent the call to voicemail. She managed to avoid him most of the day. Until she decided how to proceed in their relationship, it was best to keep their conversations minimal. At this point, she was just going through the motions. She knew it was cowardly but figured it would be better than having her heart dragged through turmoil so soon after her last breakup.

Drew's dinner was scheduled to happen at the same time as her NYAA meeting. She hoped the meeting would distract her from thinking about Drew sitting across the table from Jade, reminiscing about their past life together. Eventually, she needed to make a choice. She would either stay with Drew and trust him or reinstate her dating hiatus. Neither option would be easy.

Alana pushed thoughts of Drew and Jade to the recesses of her mind and refocused on the work in front of her. Six o'clock came before she knew it. Cadence was at her door.

"Ready to go?"

"Whoa. Look at you all ready for a NYAA meeting."

"Don't tempt me. I'm still not into all these gatherings, but I realize it's been good for business so I'm sticking with it. Just don't ask me to join the board. I like to leave the politics to my dad."

"I'm ready." Alana closed her laptop and grabbed her purse.

Chapter 24

Drew whipped the rented convertible Jaguar into the parking lot of the office where his second meeting was being held. Pressing the button, the top closed over him, cutting off the beaming rays of that California sun. When he stepped out in his blue tailored suit, he felt like was on a movie set. Several women walking through the parking lot stopped their conversations and looked his way. Drew looked back and smiled. Those grown women actually giggled.

Looking good and feeling great, he floated into the building that housed Sherwood Entertainment as if he had clouds for shoes, halting a few more conversations by the time he made it to the reception desk. Jade was to meet him there.

Jade's proposal had sounded good when she presented it at dinner the other night, but the excitement truly kicked in when those connections she boasted about started requesting meetings. Retiring his motorcycle didn't seem so grim in light of all the new opportunities that he didn't realize could exist for him. Until recently, he had never imagined transitioning into television. Most of the racers he knew stayed in the field, but the options, based on what he knew now, were limited.

Flashing a brilliant smile, he greeted the receptionist. She gushed and offered him coffee, tea or water while he waited for his other party. He politely declined. He pretended not to see the glances she stole his way as she called the producer of the show that he was there to meet.

"As soon as your other party comes, I'll take you right in," she promised.

"Thank you."

She smiled hard.

Jade walked in just as he was about to take a seat.

"Don't you look handsome?"

"You seem surprised. Didn't I look good in my jeans and motorcycle jacket?"

"Of course you did, Drew. I just don't see you like this often."

Drew chuckled. "You look pretty good yourself," he complimented her. Jade had always been very mindful of fitness. Her curves were well-placed in the dress she wore in the same shade as her name. She'd always been a beautiful woman, but Alana had his heart. It would take a lot more than a pretty face to cause him to lose focus. It was too late for that now.

The receptionist advised that Mr. Jacobson was ready to see them.

"After you." Drew stepped aside for Jade to enter first.

"You always were a gentleman," Jade said.

"And I always will be."

The receptionist led them through a modern office that

had a sea of white cubicles with glass partitions giving the workplace a futuristic feel. Posters depicting stars and popular shows produced by the network lined the walls. They entered the glassed-in conference room and greeted Mr. Jacobson and two other gentlemen.

"Archie!" Jade said with a familiarity that showed Drew that Jade had a pretty solid connection with this man. They embraced.

"You know Daniel and Mat, right?"

"Great seeing you again, gentlemen." Jade shook their hands. "This is your next hot personality, Drew Barrington."

"Gentlemen." Drew greeted the men with handshakes before they all sat.

"Let's get right to business," Archie Jacobson began. "The package you sent us was quite impressive. You have a great look and I think you may be a fit for one of the new shows we're working on. It's reality TV."

Drew wasn't excited about reality TV but continued to hear him out.

"The show follows the lives of several athletes across different sports. It's unconventional in the sense that we don't seek out drama, but rather we want to show the world what goes into the making of an athlete. You see, we know what happens on the field, but the public always wants to know what's happening when the cameras aren't flashing. We're in the process of auditioning several well-known players in different sports."

It wasn't exactly what Drew had in mind, but, then again, he didn't know what to expect. He leaned forward, being sure to remain poised. "What's the offer?"

The man who was introduced as Daniel slid a folder in front of Drew and Jade. They scanned the contents briefly.

"Not bad." Jade nodded. "Give us a few days to absorb this and we'll get back to you."

"That's fine with me." Archie looked at his colleagues. They agreed and the meeting was over.

Outside, Drew walked Jade to her car. The opportunity to be a spokesperson for the American-based motorcycle racing organization they had met with earlier seemed great. However, this reality-TV gig paid much more and offered broader exposure. Drew had several more meetings over the next week to examine his options before determining which route to take.

They agreed to finish their discussion over lunch at a restaurant that a friend recommended on North La Cienega Boulevard.

He went back to the hotel and spent the rest of the afternoon on the phone. The first thing he did was call Alana to share the news. She seemed excited enough. Drew understood that she was still uneasy about the time he had to spend with Jade handling business. He wanted to assure Alana that this transition would be great for them since he would spend much more time in the States.

"I want to know what you think about this."

"It sounds like a great opportunity." Alana sounded dejected.

"It is, *ma belle*, and we'll get to spend much more time together. Join me for my next race." Maybe having her around would help her understand that she had nothing to worry about when it came to Jade.

"I really can't."

"Then meet me in California. We can do something after my meetings."

"I won't able to take time off for a few weeks."

"Then I'll plan something special as soon as I get back." He couldn't wait to see her and intended to show her just how much he'd missed her and to make up for all of this lost time.

Next, Drew updated his brothers on his progress and asked about his dad's progress. Then he looked up a few lounges on his cell phone.

Content about his day, Drew put on some music, showered and changed into jeans, a button-down shirt, shoes and a sports jacket. He wanted to hang for the night and celebrate his prospects. He was used to being alone and taking in whatever the locals offered. However, before he could leave, Jade showed up at his door.

"You're going out?"

"I don't get to see LA as often as I used to, so I figured I'll see what's happening around town."

"By yourself? I'd be happy to join you. I mean, if you don't mind. I don't have anything to do. I was stopping by to see if you wanted to have dinner."

Drew hesitated a moment. "Sure." He wondered what harm it could do. He was loyal to Alana.

"Cool. I know just the place. Give me a moment to change my clothes. I'll be right back." Jade ran off to her room down the hall.

A little while later, she returned in a little black dress that hugged her curves tighter than his motorcycle did on race days.

Drew mentally chided Jade for her choice of dress and decided to make it clear where he stood.

"Jade." He entered the hallway, closing his hotel door behind him.

"What's up, Drew?"

"I just want to make sure we are on the same page."

"About what?"

"Where we stand. Our relationship is a professional one. I respect what you do and, in fact, I'm pretty excited about the options being presented for me, but I need you to understand that my heart is with Alana. I just didn't want there to be any misunderstandings."

Jade stood quietly for a moment. "Of course, Drew. It's all about the business." Her smile failed to reach her eyes. "We'll talk business and make this a business dinner to make you feel comfortable if that's what you want to do."

Following her recommendation, they ended up at an exclusive restaurant and lounge not far from where they'd had lunch.

"Let's dance." Jade suggested after they had eaten and enjoyed a few drinks. Jade stood, teetered and caught her balance. She pulled down the hemline of her dress.

"Maybe later." He sipped his cognac, bobbing his head to the music.

"Come on, Drew. Don't leave me hanging. We've worked hard today."

After a little more pleading Drew relented, pushed back his seat and rose slowly. He took the hand she held out and walked to the dance floor.

The last time he remembered dancing was at the party his brothers had thrown for him. Now, they danced through a few pop songs until Jade complained about the balls of her feet feeling like she'd been walking on coals. They returned to their table and listened to a few more songs while Drew finished his drink, and then they both headed back to the hotel. Drew enjoyed himself and had his fill.

As a gentleman should, he walked Jade to her room. She fumbled with her key card at the door, unable to get it into the slot. Drew took the key and opened the door for her.

Jade stood in the doorway and smiled. "Tonight was great. I needed that."

"Good."

"Do you want to come in for a little while?" Jade asked. Her words dragged.

"I'm going to head straight to bed. I'll see you in the morning."

Jade looked disappointed, but then her expression changed to something unreadable.

"Are you okay?"

"I'm fine but would be better if you hung out with me for a bit longer." In the next moment, Jade had wrapped her arms around Drew's neck, lifted on her toes and kissed him on the lips.

Drew pulled back. "Jade."

"What's wrong?" she whined, becoming instantly irritated. "You can't tell me you don't find me attractive anymore. I've seen the way you've looked at me since we've been here."

"I thought I made it clear to you earlier that our relationship here is stictly business. I've shown you nothing but respect from the beginning and I expect the same in return." Drew was surprised by Jade's approach and considered her behavior as unbecoming.

Jade sidled up to him and placed both hands on his chest. "She doesn't look like she's woman enough for you, Drew. You need someone who can fly with you—a woman with a similar taste for adventure. You need me, Drew. We were good together."

"Exactly. We *were*…" Drew removed her hands and backed up, putting space between them.

"Don't act like you don't want me." She sauntered over to him again. "Don't you remember how much fun we had together? It can be like that again." She slid her finger across his lips.

Drew moved back again and shook his head. He turned to leave her room.

"Drew! Wait! I'm sorry. I shouldn't have done that." She ran her hands through her tousled hair. "Don't go. Let's talk."

"Other than business, there's nothing to talk about. I appreciate what you've done so far and will understand if you no longer want me to be your client."

Drew headed down the hall. Jade went after him, but he kept walking.

"I'm sorry." She stepped around him, so she could stand face-to-face. "I shouldn't have done that. I never mix business… I just thought—"

"You thought I was the old Drew, but I'm not."

"I see that." Jade looked away, seeming embarrassed. "There's no need to find another company. I'll still represent you."

"Then you need to understand what I'm here for."

"I do."

"I appreciate that. See you in the morning." He walked away, leaving her in the hallway.

"Drew!" she called after him. He stopped walking but didn't turn around. "You must love her."

Drew continued walking. He didn't answer her question aloud, but he did acknowledge it in his heart.

Chapter 25

Alana spotted her parents immediately after she rounded the curve in Terminal B at LaGuardia Airport. Evelyn stood curbside with the posture of a ballerina, shielding her eyes from the gleam of the evening sun. Towering next to her was Larry, Alana's father, who became more handsome with age. His perfectly blended salt-and-pepper goatee gave him a distinguished look.

Alana blew the horn as she pulled up and then jumped out of the car. "Hey!" she sang. "How was your trip? Did you find something?" she asked, referring to their retirement home search.

"I think we did." Evelyn shimmied before hugging Alana.

"We still have a few places to see before we make a final decision. How are you, baby girl?" Larry asked.

"We can talk about it over dinner." Alana popped the trunk. Larry piled their bags inside. "Feeling like a little Peruvian fare tonight?"

"Yes. Let's go to Pio Pio on Northern since we're over here. I can't wait to tell you all about this place." Evelyn could hardly sit still.

Larry opened the passenger door to let his wife in. "You go ahead and sit in the front so you ladies can talk."

As they rode, Evelyn told Alana all about the beautiful condominiums they had visited that had overlooked the water in Puerto Rico, comparing them to those they had visited in Costa Rica and Saint Martin. Evelyn spoke fast—one sentence slid into the next, leaving no room for breaks. She was so excited Alana barely got a word in during the ride to the restaurant or during dinner.

When Alana finally dropped them off, she stayed at their house for a while just soaking up their presence. Because of her parents' trips and her relationship with Drew, she hardly spent any quality time with them.

Larry hauled their luggage up the stairs, leaving Alana and her mother in the kitchen.

"Alana, where's Drew these days?" Evelyn asked as she filled the kettle for her nightly tea.

Why did her mother have to bring him up? "He's away." Her response was dry.

"Where is he this time?" She retrieved two cups from the cabinet and set one in front of Alana.

Away with his ex-girlfriend. "In LA on business." Alana was suddenly uninterested in having tea.

"That's nice. The two of you have been spending a lot of time together lately. Looks like things are getting pretty serious between the two of you." Evelyn leaned on the countertop, awaiting details with an anxious smile.

Alana forced a smile. Normally, she would indulge her mom and the two of them would sip tea and swap stories for hours. Alana didn't feel like talking anymore.

Yawning, she got up from the stool she sat on. "It's

getting late." She looked at her watch and stretched her arms. "I need to go to bed so I can get up for work in the morning."

Evelyn must have sensed her avoidance. "You're right. It is getting late. You go ahead and rest. We've got a few more days before we have to leave again," she said, walking over to give her a hug.

"I should have followed you two into academia. You two get way too much time off," Alana teased.

"There's still time. You could teach law," Evelyn said matter-of-factly.

"I still might do it—one day." She kissed her mom and jogged upstairs to say goodbye to her father before heading to the car.

As soon as Alana climbed in and started the engine, her phone chirped. She checked and found a few missed calls from Drew and a couple of text messages. She felt horrible about avoiding him. However, he hadn't let up on her. Drew still called several times a day. When she didn't pick up, he'd fill her in on how his day had gone via text. She always knew where he was and what was happening.

From the text messages, she learned how well his trip to California was going. Alana was genuinely happy for him but annoyed at the fact that his excitement came by way of Jade Donnelly.

Pushing aside her prejudice, she dialed him back.

"Hello."

Alana pulled the phone from her ear and looked at the display to make sure she had dialed the right number. She put the phone back to her ear and said, "Hello."

"Can I help you?" the woman asked.

"Jade?" Alana questioned, though she knew it had to be.

"Yes. Who's calling? Is this Alana? Drew's busy. I can tell him you called."

Instead of responding, Alana just hung up. She jerked the car in gear and drove home faster than she should have. It was fortunate that the police weren't on the prowl because she'd broken various traffic laws.

Alana fumbled with the keys as she tried to open the front door. When she finally got inside, she tossed her jacket in one direction and her purse in the other and marched upstairs. She flopped on the bed and sat there for several moments, trying to calm her breathing.

Just as she had suspected, Jade was up to more than she had let on. Alana had sensed it at the dinner. Painful memories and possibilities flooded her mind. Had Jade and Drew slept together while they were away? Were they sharing a room? Drew had asked if Alana wanted to come with him to California. Was that a trick because he knew she was too busy to take off? Were old sparks being rekindled into fresh new flames?

Alana's eyes stung with the threat of tears, but she refused to let them fall. She was already deciding to leave so now she had a solid reason, but she wasn't sure if she really wanted to. She cared about Drew more than she wanted to admit. The past few months had been magical—the trips, the adventures and so much more. Drew had done so much to make her feel special and now she wished he hadn't done any of those things. He'd opened her up, chipped away at the fortress she built around her heart just to crush it.

She thought about calling back to see if Jade would answer again but decided against it. What could she do from three thousand miles away if she did answer besides become more upset? She thought about texting him to find out what was going on. What if Jade read the text?

Alana didn't want to give Jade the satisfaction of knowing that she had riled her.

She had some sharp and colorful words for Drew, but they would have to wait until the next time he called because she vowed never to dial his number again. She had to let go. The sting of betrayal helped make her decision. There was no need to wait for the proverbial boom to come crashing down on her. It would only be more devastating. Jade could have Drew back for all she cared. She was officially done.

Chapter 26

Yes, Drew loved Alana. He was finally putting a tag on what he had felt for a long time. It was love. He didn't *like her a lot*. He didn't *really care about her*. It was clear. It took Jade's statement for him to simply acknowledge it.

Drew intended to let Alana know how he felt today. After his meetings with a popular sports network, he wanted to stop in and surprise her. He called Cadence to make sure that Alana would be in the office around lunchtime. Alana hadn't answered his calls or responded to his texts in two days. He was going to find out why and fix whatever was broken between them.

"What's up, soon-to-be sister-in-law?"

"Not much, Drew. Are you in town?" Cadence replied.

"Just for a little while. I leave again tonight."

"I have to say, it's been great seeing so much of you. Usually, once you leave for the season, we don't get to see you for months at a time."

"Blame it on your buddy."

"I guess she does deserve partial blame."

"Is she in the office today?"

"Yep."

"Okay. She's a little upset with me, but I plan to fix all of that today."

"You're going to need heavy-duty tools."

"What makes you say that?"

"I'll let her tell you."

"Okay. Do me a favor. Don't tell her that I'm coming, but also don't let her leave. I have a meeting in midtown later and should be able to make it to your office by one. I need to speak to her about something really important. Can you do that for me, sis?"

"I'll try my best. Alana can be pretty stubborn at times."

"You're telling me. Thanks for always advocating for me. Alana is a tough girl to schmooze."

"Clear-cut honesty has always worked best with her."

"You're right. See you later."

Drew ended that call feeling good. He wasn't sure he would have gotten far with Alana if it hadn't been for Cadence rooting for him.

Jade was meeting him in midtown for his second meeting with the sports network. Watching her work had taught him a lot about her business and how to negotiate these deals. Things were a little awkward since the incident at the hotel, but Jade hadn't made any other advances. After a few more meetings and possible negotiations, he could move on without her. But, for now, he was stuck with her as she had managed to secure some major appointments that could prove to be life-changing for him.

Dressed in a dapper gray suit, Drew intended to impress the producers at the sports network. The opportunity involved hosting a show that featured extreme sports, which was perfect for such an adventurous spirit. He was also exploring a few more gigs as a spokesperson for several sports-related brands, including a helmet manufacturer. Life after racing looked much more promising to him these days.

Drew arrived at the meeting early, set his charm meter on high and wowed everyone in the boardroom. He headed back to Manhattan for his second appointment with seconds to spare.

"Drew!" Jade called out to him as he entered the lobby of the towering glass building on Sixth Avenue.

He jogged in her direction. "Hey."

Jade looked at her watch. "You're right on time. I was afraid you were going to be late." She stopped walking and tried to fix his tie. "How did your other meeting go?"

Politely, Drew moved her hands. "Very well." He stepped aside for Jade to enter the crowded elevator first. They stopped their conversation until they reached their floor.

"I still think you should have let me join you for that other meeting. I could probably get you more money if they offer you the opportunity."

"Thanks, but I think I did well."

A tall woman with broad shoulders greeted Jade at the reception desk. "I was just coming out to see if you were here." They embraced. "How are you?"

"I'm well, Victoria. You're looking good." Jade turned to acknowledge Drew. "This is Drew Barrington." Jade held his arm.

"It's a pleasure to meet you." Victoria scanned him from head to toe. Her grin made Drew feel like she wanted to have him for lunch.

"The pleasure's all mine." They shook and Drew gave her a polite nod. He glanced at Jade just in time to see the hint of a covetous smirk fall from her face.

"Well, let's get started." Victoria led them through frosted-glass doors behind the reception desk into a room of several other women.

Once again, Drew paid close attention to how Jade handled the meeting with Victoria, taking mental notes. She was good at her job and always demanded the best options.

Even as he gleaned knowledge from Jade, he couldn't help but think about Alana. He couldn't wait to get to her office.

Victoria communicated her interest in working with Drew.

"So what are the next steps?" Jade asked, obviously anxious to move forward.

"I just want to make sure you understand," Drew interjected. "I will have limited availability until my current contract ends next year."

Victoria and her team assured him that wouldn't be a problem. "As long as we have your schedule we can work that out. Your endorsements will be helpful, as well," Victoria said.

"Thanks so much for your time." Drew stood. "I'm going to review all the information and get back to you with my decision."

No one else stood or moved. Victoria looked to Jade and her staff and then back at Drew.

"You're not ready to move forward?" She looked confused.

"Today? I'm extremely excited about this, but I just want to consider a few things first. I've been presented with quite a few opportunities. I'd like a little time to know that I'm making the best decision."

Victoria lifted from her seat. She was obviously disappointed. "Sure, I can understand that, but I assure you that we are ready to have you begin representing our clothing line right away. We're at the top of our game in this business."

"Thank you. It was truly a pleasure, ladies." He offered handshakes all around and flashed one more gleaming smile. Suddenly, he couldn't wait to leave the office. Pulling his suit jacket together, he strutted out the boardroom door.

A moment later, Jade scurried out behind him, catching him as he entered the elevator.

"I think we should definitely sign with this company, Drew. They can really get you into the spotlight. I thought that would happen today." Jade sounded disappointed.

"This seems great. I just don't want to jump in too fast. We have more appointments and I really want to explore all of my first."

"Sure, after our next set of meetings overseas, you should be in a better position to make that call," Jade agreed.

When the doors finally opened, Jade hurried off. "I'll call you later about the meetings we have lined up in Spain next week."

"Okay. See you then." Drew hailed a taxi and gave him the address to Alana's office. He texted Cadence when he arrived at the building to make sure Alana was there. He ran inside the drugstore up the block and picked the best batch of flowers he could find to accompany the beautiful diamond earrings and matching pendant he had for Alana.

Bouncing off the elevator, Drew strutted through their offices with a song in his heart. He saw Cadence first.

"Drew."

"What's up, sis? Where's Alana?"

"Well..." Cadence wrung her hands.

"What's wrong, Cadence?"

Before she could respond, Alana walked out of her office, stopped when she saw Drew and then looked away.

"Hello," she greeted him with a cool tone. She handed a folder to Jennifer and asked her to file it before walking back into her office.

"What just happened?" Drew questioned. A gang of thoughts rumbled through his mind. Alana was obviously more upset with him than he realized. He had to find a way to fix this.

Drew stepped into Alana's office. She stood facing the window and didn't turn around when he entered.

"Hey." There had to be more going on than just Alana being upset about him working with Jade. At this point that wasn't anything new.

Drew could see Alana's back lift and fall from the deep breaths she inhaled and exhaled. Finally, she turned around and began to speak.

"I have had a wonderful time over the past few months—magical even, but..."

Drew stepped closer. "But what?"

"I realize this is just not going to work. I'm not ready for all of this. I don't think you are either."

Drew reared his head back. She obviously had no idea how ready he truly was.

She continued in spite of his reaction. "I think it's best that we...go our separate ways."

Confusion masked his face. Drew attempted to speak,

but the words jumbled. "Separate ways? Is this why you haven't called or returned my calls in days?"

"I'm sorry, Drew. I really do wish you well." Alana turned to the window, giving him her back.

"Wish me well? Alana!"

"Please don't." She didn't turn around. "This was hard enough."

"Is there something you're not telling me?"

At first, Alana didn't respond. "I'm sorry. I need to get back to work."

There was so much more to say, but the words wouldn't come together properly. Drew took in a sharp breath before continuing. "That's not good enough for me, Alana. What's really going in here?"

"I can't talk about this now. Not here."

"If not here and now, then where and when? The least you could do is give me a concrete reason why all of the sudden you believe this can't work. What has changed in the past two days?" Drew felt his chest heave. Drew knew Alana wasn't being completely honest. There was more under the surface.

"I can't go into this here at my office. This is not the time."

Alana had a point. This wasn't a conversation that should be had at work, especially when he became more upset with each passing moment. Drew turned to wrench the doorknob and paused. Gently, he turned the knob and walked out. The joy he'd felt all day had been siphoned from him in the small amount of time since he had arrived.

Cadence was waiting outside Alana's office. Her face was drawn, showing how upset she was by all of this, as well. Drew could clearly see Cadence's pain. She wanted this to work as much as he did. She hugged him and stepped aside so he could leave.

Wading through a storm of emotions, he finally credited himself for doing what he could to make a relationship between them work. Was there a way to salvage this? Maybe he needed to give Alana some time. Then he thought about just giving up.

Drew pulled out the gift box from his jacket pocket and placed the earrings and pendant on the floor outside her office. He wrote her a short note. Drew looked at Alana's closed door one more time, shook his head and left.

Chapter 27

"Come in," Alana replied to the soft knock on her door. Quickly, she wiped away the tears rolling down her face. Saying goodbye to Drew was one of the hardest things she'd ever had to do, but it was necessary.

"Are you okay?"

Alana sat straight. "I'm fine."

Cadence sat across from her desk, reached over and put her hand over Alana's.

Alana hoped Cadence hadn't felt the slight tremble in her hand. She was far from okay. She'd just told Drew to leave her alone. She'd come to love him in a way that she didn't know was possible. Now she questioned her actions. Then she thought about Jade's voice on the phone when she called and all the speculation that action generated. Her heart and mind had been flipping and flopping for days now. She justified her actions and then questioned them almost immediately.

Alana hadn't bothered telling Drew about the call because she assumed he'd deny any kind of betrayal. Maybe she should have been more adamant and insisted that Drew not work with Jade at all, but it wouldn't have been fair for her insecurities to cost him potential opportunities. Drew didn't like the fact that she had taken Gary on for a client, but he respected her decision anyway. They thought Gary had been good for business, even though he was such a difficult client.

It was over now. Hopefully Drew wouldn't push the issue too much. Walking away was painful enough. Knowing he was leaving later that night made her appreciate his impending distance.

Cadence continued holding Alana's hand in silence, letting her wrestle with her emotions without interruption, just like a friend does.

"Aren't you glad that Gary finally listened to us and decided to settle the case?" Cadence asked, breaking the silence. "He flushed his chances of winning down the toilet when he lost it in the courtroom."

"This will be best for all of us." Alana welcomed the change of subject, but it was hard to think of anything else. She was livid when Jade answered Drew's phone and had been angry ever since.

What Alana didn't expect was to almost fall apart when she saw Drew. When she looked into his face, she felt wounded and wanted answers to questions she couldn't bring herself to ask. She couldn't trust herself to speak more than a few words at a time lest she break down right in front of him and she couldn't do that—especially not at work.

Listening to him leave ripped her apart emotionally. She couldn't bring herself to actually watch him walk out of her life. Now, she questioned herself again. Should she have given him a chance to tell his side? He didn't look like he was there to apologize. When she came out of the office, he had seemed his usual self. Alana decided an apology wouldn't have made a difference. She still needed to go for her own sake. Dating so soon after her breakup with James wasn't smart.

Worst of all, Drew had the nerve to look impossibly handsome. Memories of the time they'd spent together inundated her mind. She remembered his kisses, his touch, the way he made love to her as if he adored her. *Ma belle.* She could still hear him whispering that in her ear. She could see the sun setting as they floated in that hot air balloon. She'd fallen for the new Drew and now she couldn't eject him from her system. She didn't know what it was that she felt for him. All she knew was that it was far more intense than anything she'd ever felt for any man.

Cadence rubbed the back of her hand, bringing Alana back to the present.

"He said he's leaving tonight for Spain."

"Okay." Alana had made a decision and was going to stick with it. The last thing she was going to do was run after him.

"I almost forgot. He left this for you." Cadence handed Alana a jewelry box and flowers.

Alana took the box and dropped it in her purse. She'd look at it later. "I'm going to be fine, Cadence."

"Can I throw in my few cents?"

Alana raised a brow at her. "If I say no, will you listen?"

"Nah."

"Go ahead." Alana sat back and braced herself for her friend's honesty. She was sure it was coming.

"No matter how scared you may be, you can't outrun your own heart."

Alana sighed.

"Trust me, I know." Cadence got up. "Why don't you go home for the rest of the day? I can handle anything that comes up in the next few hours. You could use the rest."

"This is one time that I have to agree with you about needing rest."

Cadence rounded Alana's desk and hugged her.

Alana's own home didn't seem as warm when she got there. In the kitchen, she sat on a stool with her elbows on the countertop. She rested her head in her hands. A few moments later, she walked to the refrigerator, opened it and scanned the shelves. Closing it again, she decided she wasn't hungry. She went to the den and the remote was on top of the couch pillow, where Drew always left it. Had she even watched TV since they'd become estranged?

She questioned her decision to come home. At work, there were more distractions and fewer reminders of Drew. She went to her study and turned on her laptop. The icon for the language app stared back at her— mocking her. Drew had purchased the program for her so that she would learn French in preparation for their next visit to his chateau. He promised to bring her in June when the lavender fields were in full bloom. In the short time that they'd become exclusive, Drew had embedded himself in her life in so many ways. He hardly spent time at his home in Brooklyn. He stayed at her house when he wasn't visiting his parents. She felt the void his absence left in her home. She'd lived alone for years but never had she felt lonely—until now.

Alana checked her purse for her cell to make sure she didn't miss any calls. She felt the gift box that Cadence said Drew had left for her when she dug in the bag for the phone. Curiosity won her over and she opened it. She inhaled.

The diamond earrings and matching pendant were exquisite. Was that an apology gift? The card fell to the floor when she pulled out the pendant. When she leaned over to pick it up, she noticed there was writing on it. She read the words—*Don't give up on us. I'm working on making you love me. Love Drew*—and she nearly dropped the box. Her eyes watered. She squeezed them shut to hold back another stream of tears. It was too late now.

Chapter 28

Drew was upset with Alana for the way she'd treated him. All his efforts to prove himself to her were futile. Now what they had was over and he couldn't fathom why. Alana didn't care for Jade, but she'd stuck it out. He'd done all he could to keep her insecurities at bay. What had changed in those few days? Of all the women who craved him, why did he have to fall for the one who could so easily toss him aside? Was this payback for being such a slippery player? Karma was paying him an unwelcome visit.

"Are you alright?" Jade asked again. She'd managed to arrange for their first-class seats to be together.

"I'm fine." Drew lost count of how many times he'd told Jade that since boarding the plane.

Once they arrived, Drew perked himself up for the meetings, media briefs and practice, but the second he left the track, he went right back to being disgruntled.

He even felt out of sorts while dining with his friends the night before the race.

Even after being away for a few days, he hadn't heard from Alana. She was serious about moving on. All of his efforts to cast thoughts of her aside failed. He'd toyed with the idea of giving up on love altogether and returning to his former ways, but he no longer desired that life. He longed to hear from her, to touch her, but the sting of rejection kept him from dialing her number. He'd almost sent her an absentminded update by text and then realized they weren't on good terms.

Tension convened in Drew's neck and shoulders. He found himself rolling that injured shoulder and massaging it to ease the tightness.

After dinner, Sean pulled him aside. "What's up with you, man?"

"What do you mean?" Drew asked.

"You're not yourself. You seem uptight. I don't want this to affect you tomorrow."

"It's just a little stress from something I had to deal with back home. I'll be alright."

"Is it your dad? I thought he was doing better."

"Yeah." Drew didn't bother expanding into the truth. He'd never told Sean about how serious he was about Alana.

"Alright, my man." Sean patted his back. "Get some rest. We've got a race to win."

When Drew got back to the hotel, Jade was waiting for him. She opened the door as he passed her room. "Hey."

Drew's greeting was a lifted chin.

"How was dinner?"

"Pretty good. I'll see you in the morning." He wasn't up for conversation.

Inside, Drew removed his clothes and climbed right

into bed. The tension was exhausting. He tried not to think of Alana, but he couldn't help himself. Nothing he did to distract himself worked. Alana invaded his thoughts on the track, at dinner and especially when Jade was around. She was a physical reminder of his discontentment when it came to Alana.

Despite everything that had happened, he still longed for Alana. He'd loved her long before he ever admitted it to himself. Drew argued with himself. Was he going to sit back and just accept what had happened or should he go after Alana one more time? His heart wasn't ready to give up, but his mind and ego urged him to move on. Drew wondered if she liked the earrings and if she'd read the note.

Drew allowed the hot shower to massage his shoulders and back. It refreshed him just a little. He stepped out of the shower, headed to the room and picked up his phone.

"I can't believe this woman infiltrated my system like this." Drew went back into the bathroom and lifted his toothbrush to his mouth. When he finished he launched one of his favorite music apps to allow soothing jazz music to help him settle down. He tried to get into the rhythm, which was part of his ritual when showering and getting dressed. Alana's absence made most things seem off-kilter. He was in awe at the amount of patience he'd exhibited with this woman.

Drew slipped into a pair of boxers and headed for bed, but once again his longing for Alana disrupted his sleep. It was the only way he could experience her. It bothered him that she had somehow planted herself in his system and as much as he tried to cut away the memory of her, Alana remained rooted in his heart. He desired her in his dreams as much as he did in reality.

His fitful night of sleep ended with the sun obnoxiously beaming across his face. He shielded his eyes before opening them fully. The dull thumping at his temple returned as it did each morning when his nights were restless. Drew threw back the covers, hopped out of bed and started the coffeemaker. After a full cup, another long shower and two Tylenols, he was ready to meet Sean in the lobby.

It was race day. He had to push dominating thoughts of Alana aside to indulge his second love. The yearning to win set his adrenaline pumping the moment he reached the track. Soaking up the energy of his friends and enthusiasts, Drew was almost himself by the time he got to the locker room. Joking with his fellow bikers and stepping into his jumpsuit brought him closer to his usual unbridled excitement.

"Hey, Sean! Careful out there, I don't want you swallowing too much of my dust," Drew teased.

Several riders hooted.

"It will be impossible for me to swallow dust from in front of you."

"This win is already mine, buddy. You better be right behind me." Drew pointed at him, teasing and encouraging him at the same time.

"See you at the finish line. Whenever you get there." Sean pumped his fist and jogged out of the locker room.

Drew and the other racers followed behind.

Winding through the usual throngs of press, staff, groupies and VIPs, they made their way to the pit. The crew looked the bike over. Inspecting the beauty, Drew caressed it with a tender touch. Mounting the bike, he kissed two gloved fingers and touched the handlebars. "This one is ours, baby girl." He felt his confidence returning. This was his element—the crowd, the noise, people yelling, announcers deliberating over the PA system. His heart pulsated a little faster. The rhythm fueled his exhilaration.

Drew coolly rode over to his starting point, adjacent to a native beauty with all of her subtle curves on display for everyone to see. He thought of Alana.

The flag dropped. Drew released the clutch and took off. The speed was thrilling. The first corner came quickly; Drew leaned in, tightened his legs and shot out of that curve like a rocket. He sprung into first place. Maintaining his lead through the first few laps, Drew glided effortlessly until another racer was at his side. Drew yanked the throttle, springing forward once again, putting distance between him and the person behind him. Another racer gained on him and then kept pace alongside him. Drew dipped his motorcycle from one side to the other, in and out of a deep series of curves.

Several laps in, cruising at 175 miles per hour, Drew's heart thumped. He boasted an assured smile behind his helmet. He'd managed to maintain his lead for more than half the race. Keeping his eye on the clear track in front of him, Drew focused on technique as he leaned into his next corner.

Two racers passed Drew. He refocused, gaining a lead over one of them. Riding neck and neck with another, he pushed to 180 miles per hour, acquiring a small lead. He felt a jolt from behind—another rider gaining on him. His motorcycle swerved and he began losing control. In an attempt to right the bike, a sharp pain sprang through his shoulder. The bike skirted across the track into the path of oncoming riders rolling at top speed. One of them crashed into him, broadsiding his motorcycle. The impact sent him into the air. When he landed, everything went black.

Chapter 29

Alana woke with a start. Propelling forward, she patted the sheets in search of her ringing cell phone. Focusing through the darkness, she squinted, noticing the time above all. It was just after five in the morning.

Why was Cadence calling her so early? Sensing that something was wrong, Alana swiped the phone. The call ended before she could answer. Taking a deep breath, Alana dialed back.

"Come on, Cadence. Pick up," she beckoned.

"Alana!" Cadence answered in a rush.

"What's going on?"

"It's Drew."

Alana's chest tightened. Cadence sounded like she'd been crying. "What about Drew? Isn't he in Barcelona?"

"He had an accident… It's bad." She sniffled.

Tears sprang to Alana's eyes and air filled her chest. She hopped out of bed not sure where she was going. She just knew she couldn't lie there anymore.

"How'd you find out?" Alana walked circles on the floor by the foot of her bed.

"Sean called Blake. Hunter is checking flights for all of us now. Mrs. Barrington is staying behind with their dad. We're leaving on the first flight available. You should come too."

Alana thought about how cold she'd been to Drew the day he left. Surely she'd be the last person he would want to see. "I don't know about that, Cadence."

"This is Drew! You have much more history with him than one incident. You may be confused about how you feel for him when it comes to your relationship, but I know that you love him as a friend and right now he needs his family and his closest friends. I need you there." Cadence broke down.

Hearing Cadence cry prompted more of Alana's tears. Sniffling replaced the words between them. Moments passed before either of them spoke.

Cadence was correct, and in more ways than she knew. Alana did love him but not just as a friend. That was why she'd acted so crazy, pulling away to avoid being hurt. She couldn't imagine enduring the pain of Drew hurting her. Jade had upset their balance when she injected herself back into their lives and fear had sent Alana cowering.

As she sat on the phone listening to Cadence cry, her chest swirled with a physical pain. The idea of losing Drew altogether was shattering. What if he didn't make it? She didn't just want to be there; she needed to be there. She'd deal with whatever happened after that.

"Send me the flight details. I'll book mine and meet you at the airport."

Alana pitched the phone back on the bed. Tearing clothes from their hangers, she stuffed a few pairs of jeans and shirts into her suitcase. She didn't know how long she'd end up staying, but it didn't matter. If a need arose, she'd deal with it there.

By the time Alana finished showering, Cadence had emailed her a copy of their flight itinerary and an e-ticket for Alana. She hadn't expected them to pay for hers too. She'd reimburse them when she arrived in Spain. Alana hauled her suitcase to the car. She texted Cadence to see where she was and met them at Blake's house.

Cadence opened the door and Alana stepped right into her arms. When Alana released Cadence, Blake was standing beside them. She hugged him too.

"I'm so sorry this happened, Blake."

Alana could tell that he was distressed by the tight set of his jaw. She couldn't remember seeing him ever look so serious.

Their flight wasn't scheduled to leave until ten that night, but once Alana had packed, she couldn't sit at home alone. She carried her restlessness to Blake's house so that she wouldn't have to endure the excruciating wait alone.

"Let's go grab something to eat," Alana suggested. She had to do something.

"That's not a bad idea," Cadence agreed. "Blake, are you up to it?"

"Yeah, let's go." Blake lifted himself off the couch as if something weighed him down. Alana was often awed by the way emotional heaviness manifested in such physical ways.

They went to the restaurant, despite none of them having much of an appetite. Sean kept them updated on Drew's condition as much as he could. Since he wasn't family, the doctors had given him little information. So far, all they knew was that Drew had been knocked unconscious during the accident, carted off the track on a stretcher and rushed to the hospital for surgery. The closer Alana got to Drew, the more anxious she became. However, turning back was not an option. She even toyed with the idea of revealing her true feelings to Drew when she got there. If she got the chance she'd let him know for sure.

They met Hunter and Chey at the airport and boarded the plane with a solemn eeriness permeating the space around them. Due to the late booking, the five of them were scattered around the plane. Flying through the night and into the next morning, they arrived in Barcelona ten and a half restless hours later. Their stopover in Dublin broke up what little sleep they had, but their anxiousness to see Drew pushed the fatigue aside.

Sean arranged for them to be picked up from the airport and brought straight to the hospital. Drew was sedated while the doctors updated Hunter and Blake on his condition. He'd successfully come through surgery, which repaired severely torn muscles and ligaments in his shoulder. His concussion would have lingering effects requiring him to take it easy for a while. Blake and Hunter went into the room to see him first and then the girls went in.

The girls held hands as they stood over Drew's bedside. Tears rolled down their cheeks as they watched Drew's chest rise and fall. Despite the mayhem surrounding the situation, he seemed to be sleeping peacefully. For several moments, the only sound in the room besides sniffles were the monitors' beeping.

Cadence touched Drew's hand. "Hey, little brother. Do you hear me?"

Chey wiped tears with the back of her finger. "Who's going to call me Dr. Smell Good?" They all chuckled.

"Yeah, who else would I be angry with?" Alana added, giving all of them a good, tearful laugh.

Later, Cadence and Chey left the room, leaving Alana alone with Drew. She stared at him for a while. Touched his nose and let her finger slide across his lips, remembering how those lips felt. She closed her eyes, sending more tears down her cheeks.

"Hurry up and wake up. There are things I need to say to you…like *I'm sorry*." Alana wiped her tears. "You became everything I ever wanted in a man, and it scared the hell out of me. I thought it couldn't be real. Then your ex came along and tried to pry you away from me and I let it happen. I'm sorry about that too. I'm not sure I know how to trust. That's something I have to learn. Maybe you could teach me. I'm no longer scared. If you're willing, give me a second chance." Alana looked to the ceiling, batting her eyes. Her emotions went awry and her attempt at collecting them failed. Taking his hand, she leaned over him and cried.

"You did it, Drew. You said you were going to make me love you, and you did. Now wake up."

Chapter 30

Drew's eyes fluttered. He tried to open them, but they seemed too heavy. After several attempts, he was able to lift his lids just a little. The light in the room assaulted his sight and he squeezed his eyes shut. Pain registered in several parts—his arm, hands, shoulders and leg. His head felt like hammers were being slammed against it in a steady rhythm.

Drew swallowed and cleared his throat, and then he peeled his lips apart. Dry mouth and a sore throat made it difficult to speak. He tried opening his eyes again. Taking his time, he adjusted to the light. He looked at the florescent lighting, pale walls and monitors. Realizing he was in the hospital, he panicked. The tempo on the monitor increased, beeping faster, adding dings and buzzes to the symphony. Drew struggled to sit up, but pain knocked inside his head and ripped through his shoulder. He cautiously laid back and took a deep breath.

Drew licked his dry lips and before he could call out

the word *nurse* as loudly as he could, one sprinted into the room.

"Mr. Barrington, I'm right here," she said in her Spanish accent. She tapped the screen of the monitor, checked the levels of the IV and leaned over to look into his eye with a small flashlight. "It's good to see you awake. Don't try to speak, okay?" The monitors quieted, returning to a singular rhythm.

The nurse left the room and, moments later, Drew heard the sound of additional feet entering. She returned with a young doctor, who spoke with a soothing voice. Her perfect English made him wonder where he was.

The doctor spoke to him the entire time she poked, prodded, checked and examined him.

"My—" Drew cleared his throat "—my family..."

"Yes, your family has arrived. They came to see you this morning, but you were resting. The pain medication and trauma from your accident can make you very drowsy. We will let them know you're up as soon as we're done here. How's your head feeling?"

Drew winced.

"Yes, you have a pretty bad concussion, but you should be thankful. That helmet saved your life. For several weeks, you'll experience headaches, dizziness, sensitivity to light, and you'll find it difficult to focus or concentrate at times, but that will all go away. You also tore your shoulder up so you had to have surgery. When you leave here, you'll need to follow up with your doctor and go to therapy for several weeks."

Drew huffed. He didn't need the doctor to tell him what that meant for racing. So much would be affected by him missing the rest of the season, but he was alive.

"If you could sit up for me." The doctor helped him lean forward as she placed a stethoscope against his bare back. "So sorry. It's a little cold," she said when he winced. "Okay," she exhaled as she guided him back against the pillow. "You're all set. You should be able to walk out of here in a few days."

"Thank you," he managed to say. The raspy voice didn't sound like his own. He cleared his throat and tried again.

"No worries, Mr. Barrington." She turned to the nurse. *"Agua."*

Drew remembered he was in Spain. Other snatches of memory came to him in flashes. He put enough of the pieces together to recall some of the accident—those few moments when he went airborne before everything turned black.

Drew lay there as time passed, trying not to become too discouraged. Eventually, he fell asleep. Familiar voices emerged in the distance. Initially, he thought he was dreaming. Squeezing his eyes, he realized the voices were outside of his head. He heard Hunter's deep voice and then Blake's. There was a woman. He wanted to flick his eyes open but had to move slowly, knowing the light would hurt. The woman sounded like Cadence. Maybe it was Chey. Then he figured he had to be dreaming because he thought he heard Alana or Jade.

"He's opening his eyes."

Drew heard the shuffle of several feet.

"Drew! Can you hear us?"

He peeled his eyes open, blinking repeatedly. Several figures came into focus. Drew nodded and swallowed. His throat was dry again.

"Thank goodness!"

That voice made him want to sit up. Squinting, he looked around the bed. *"Ma belle."*

Jade stepped up. "I'm here, Drew." She cupped his hand in hers.

That wasn't the voice he'd heard a moment ago. "Alana?" he croaked, cleared his throat and called her again. "Where's Alana?" he whispered. Jade dropped his hand.

"I'm over here, Drew."

Alana came into view. The air suddenly seemed fresh. Drew took a deep breath and then managed a weak smile. *"Ma belle,"* he whispered and puckered his lips. Alana leaned over, kissed him and rested her forehead against his. *"Je t'aime, ma belle."*

Alana laughed and cried simultaneously against his temple.

"I told you I was going to make you love me," he whispered. "And I love you too." That was all that mattered.

Chapter 31

"Drew, you're not helping!" Alana shrieked.

"I'm helping me," he teased, pressing himself against Alana's backside as she tried to brush her teeth. Drew spun her around to face him, kissed her forehead, cheeks, chin and nose before moving to her lips.

"We're going to be late," she protested without putting up much resistance.

"So?" He kissed her again.

Alana couldn't help but get lost in the series of tender kisses he planted on her lips.

"You love me?"

"Yes, I love you, Drew." Alana gave him a quick peck and ducked under his arm. She turned back to the bathroom mirror and finally began brushing.

As terrifying as his accident was, Alana was thankful for what had come of it. While he was still in the hospital, they cleared the air. Drew needed to understand what had made Alana give up on him. She told him how upset she was when Jade answered his phone. Drew was surprised because he hadn't been aware of that. He briefly recalled leaving his phone in the suite while he went to his room to retrieve a folder for a meeting during one of their trips. Jade had never mentioned the fact that Alana had called and Drew had never checked his phone to see that he had missed her call.

Angry at Jade's antics, he got Jade on the phone to confront her, but she hung up when she realized that Alana was right there with him. Jade headed back to the States and they hadn't heard from her since. Alana apologized for being such a difficult girlfriend. Drew apologized to her for making her doubt him. Together they agreed to start fresh.

Drew was strong enough to return home two weeks after his release from the hospital. When he arrived in the States, Alana nursed him back to health. Several months later, they returned to France for a quick vacation before Drew was due to start his new job as a commentator with the sports network.

Drew watched Alana brush her teeth. He was so into her that the simplest gesture could turn him on. "Just one more time." The sultry look in Drew's eyes accompanied by his naughty grin almost coaxed Alana into giving in. She'd already taken two showers and noon hadn't arrived yet.

They had practically been in each other's arms since they arrived at the chateau a few nights before. Drew woke her up with kisses, making love to her before the sun rose, casting its morning glow through his country home's windows. After their first shower, Alana moisturized her body with a sweet-smelling oil that Drew had picked up in Paris when they first arrived. Knowing that he was watching, Alana sensually rubbed the lotion into her bare skin. By the time she'd reached her feet, Drew had stepped out of his clothes, lifted her in the air and carried her to the bed. He feasted on her before driving them to a quick release. Their appetite for one another was intense, never fully sated. With short breaks, they could go on loving each other for hours.

"Okay, I'll leave you alone. We need to get going."

"What's the name of the place again?" Alana asked innocently, rinsing her toothbrush.

"I never told you the name and I'm not going to. It's a surprise, remember?"

Alana giggled. She'd been trying to get him to reveal details about his plans for days, but he refused.

Once they were fully dressed, they mounted Jolie, the bike that Drew kept at his home in France. Alana had expected him to avoid bikes after the accident, but once he'd received clearance from his doctor, he returned to his other love but rode with caution. The industry still showed great respect for him and he was asked to become the spokesperson for one of their top helmet manufacturers, making commercials about how the helmet had saved his life. It even featured clips from his accident, which rocked the industry.

Drew and Alana cruised along the countryside, passing lavender blossoms and vineyards. Alana loved the feeling of wind blowing through her hair as they rode. Occasionally, she'd hold her hand out to catch the breeze. She wrapped her arms around Drew's body and rested her head against his back. On flat surfaces, the vibration of the bike soothed her. As they rode over cobbled streets, they would open their mouths saying "Ah!" and listen to how the bumps made their voices tremble, acting like children. Then they would release joyous laughter into the air.

Drew pulled into one of the vineyards and parked the bike. The engine settled as they climbed off.

"Oh, Drew! We're doing the wine tasting today. Yes!" She threw her fist in the air. Alana's excitement bubbled.

Loving Drew was fun, satisfying and sometimes wild. His primary residence was now the penthouse in Manhattan, which was close to her and his fascinating new job at the sports network. He'd also accepted several other opportunities as a commentator. Requests to host shows outside the racing field came consistently.

"Yes, we're going to taste some wine, among other things." Drew lifted his brow and winked.

"You're so fresh."

"I actually wasn't trying to be fresh that time, but you'll see."

They walked into a shop near the entrance of the winery. Drew introduced himself to the woman behind the counter and she instructed him to follow her. Taking Alana by the hand, Drew led the way down a corridor into a gourmet kitchen.

"Your chef will be with you shortly. You can change here."

"Change? Drew, what are we doing?"

He only smiled.

The chef came and greeted them in French and handed them aprons. Alana proudly responded in French. The online lessons that Drew had purchased worked.

The chef pulled out several ingredients, and when Alana realized they were there to make chocolate, she gasped. "Drew! This is so exciting. How did you think of this?"

"You love chocolate. We both love wine. I figured this would be a perfect combination."

They spent the next hour indulging in their chocolate-making lesson and smearing the cocoa on each other's lips just to kiss it off. Leaving their chocolate to settle in their molds, they toured the winery, choosing wines to pair with their sweets.

Later, they took their chocolate and two bottles of wine and strapped it down on the back of the bike.

They passed a village with quaint shops and eateries. Drew pulled the bike over, and they walked hand in hand through the streets.

"Let's go in here. I saw something that would look good in the house."

Alana followed him inside and greeted the gentleman in front with a warm smile. The gallery was narrow but long with large windows that allowed light to pour inside. Alana loved the abstract artwork on display in the first section. She walked toward the rear and halted.

"What?" Alana covered her mouth in shock as she continued toward the large photographs of her and Drew from their impromptu photo shoot on her last visit to France. She'd forgotten all about it. Truthfully, she never expected anything to come out of those pictures, but looking at them now, some were hot, others were fun and a few were downright sexy. She could see herself hanging some in her living room.

"I think I'd like to buy one of these," Drew joked.

She snaked her arm around his waist and looked up into his sparkling eyes. "You love surprising me, don't you?" she asked. Drew nodded.

"I like the way you look in these pictures, especially that one." Drew pointed.

Alana looked in that direction and noticed one of the sexy pictures they'd taken that day and smiled. She and Drew straddled the bike, facing each other as Drew leaned toward her with his hands strategically placed across her torso. She loved it.

"You know what, sir? We'll take them all," Drew announced.

The gentleman joined them at the rear. "Shall we have them shipped to the chateau?" he asked.

It was then that Alana noticed that it was the same photographer who had taken the pictures. He and Drew laughed at her surprised expression when she put it all together. Drew managed to make her feel like a princess.

After a quick sit-down for dessert, Drew and Alana hopped back on the bike and returned to his house. The sun had begun to make a remarkable descent as they reached home—casting variations of orange along the horizon. They carried the two bottles of wine and the chocolates into the kitchen. Drew took Alana by the hand and led her to the enclosed patio out back. Alana switched on the light and screamed.

"Surprise!" their family and friends yelled together.

Bent over with one hand over her heart and one covering her mouth, Alana laughed. Cadence, Blake, Chey, Hunter, Mr. and Mrs. Barrington and her own parents were all there, laughing too. After she hugged everyone, she spun around to scold Drew for almost scaring the life out of her. When she turned, he was down on one knee.

Alana's breath caught and tears rolled down her face. Drew stood with the largest and most beautiful heart-shaped diamond she'd ever seen.

He stared into her glistening eyes. "We've been through so much. I found out what it was like to experience life without you and decided it's better with you by my side. Now that I've made you love me, will you—"

"Yes!" she yelled. "Of course, I'll marry you!"

Alana jumped into his arms. He lifted her, swinging her around. Everyone in the room cheered. Drew put her down and their lips connected. It felt like they were the only ones in the room.

Someone cleared his throat and they finally tore themselves away from each other. Everyone laughed all over again. Drew placed the ring on her finger. Alana admired it, holding her hand high.

"Let me see!" Cadence ran over to look at Alana's ring. Chey was right behind her.

Alana held her hand out, presenting her prized jewel.

"Oh! That. Is. Beautiful," Chey said.

"Come here, Evelyn. Let's go inspect this thing." Joyce waved Alana's mother over. The fathers gave each other a quick glance and chuckled.

"Hmm." Joyce examined the ring first and held Alana's hand toward her mother.

"I see…" Evelyn peered over her glasses, turning Alana's finger from one side to the other. Alana set her other hand on her hip, sniggering at their mothers.

They looked at each other. "He did well," they said at the same time and burst into laughter.

"Did someone say it was party time?" Blake held up a bottle of champagne.

"That's what I heard," Hunter added with his hand behind his ear.

For the first time since entering the patio, Alana noticed the table full of food and drinks.

"Blake, put our song on," Drew yelled over the chatter.

"You've got it, baby brother."

Seconds later, "I'm Gonna Make You Love Me" by the Supremes filled the room. Blake moved the furniture back, creating space for a dance floor. Everyone took their lovers by the hand and danced to Drew and Alana's theme song.

"You won't get away again," Drew declared.

"I don't plan on going anywhere." Alana lifted onto her toes. Drew leaned down toward her and they rubbed noses.

Once again, their lips connected in a sweet lock. Alana had finally found her prince.

* * * * *

REQUEST YOUR FREE BOOKS!

2 FREE NOVELS PLUS 2 FREE GIFTS!

KIMANI™ ROMANCE

Love's ultimate destination!

KROM1

JUST CAN'T GET ENOUGH?

Join our social communities
and talk to us online.

You will have access to the latest
news on upcoming titles and special
promotions, but most importantly,
you can talk to other fans about your
favorite Harlequin reads.

Harlequin.com/Community

Facebook.com/HarlequinBooks

Twitter.com/HarlequinBooks

Pinterest.com/HarlequinBooks

SPECIAL EXCERPT FROM

HARLEQUIN

*Summer Dupree has high hopes for the new
Bare Sophistication lingerie boutique slated for a
grand opening in Miami. Then she spies a familiar face.
Up-and-coming fashion photographer Aiden Chase
brings back cherished—and painful—memories.
And now her childhood confidant isn't letting Summer
slip away again. He's ready to create a future together.
Even when an unexpected threat resurfaces, Aiden
won't give up this time without a fight. Can he turn his
long-simmering passion for Summer into a love story
for the ages?*

*Read on for a sneak peek at
WAITING FOR SUMMER, the next exciting
installment in author Sherelle Green's
BARE SOPHISTICATION series!*

As he approached, she was able to cast her eyes across
his face more closely. Aaliyah had described him as milk
chocolate, but Summer had to slightly disagree. She'd
spent most of her life admiring Aiden's complexion and
it was definitely more like a piece of rich caramel dipped
in hazelnut. His strong jawline, deep eyes and low, neatly
trimmed beard took his look from sexy to downright
delicious. Not that she was thinking about her friend as

KPEXP1016

delicious. She was just observing a known fact… Or so she kept telling herself.

When he finally stood in front of her, he didn't say anything. She felt his eyes on every part of her face, which caused her cheeks to grow warmer by the second. *Girl, get ahold of yourself.* This was Aiden. Her old classmate Aiden. Her good friend Aiden. He must have sensed her discomfort because he finally broke the silence.

"There are no better days than summer days," he said with a smile, causing Summer to laugh harder than she'd intended. Hearing him say those words brought her back to her first day of kindergarten. She'd laughed then. She laughed now.

"Well, those *are* the best days," she replied as she leaned in to give him a hug. Just like that, the feeling of discomfort dimmed. It didn't go away, but it definitely lowered. She ignored the butterflies she felt in her stomach when they embraced and instead relished the joy of seeing her longtime friend.

Don't miss WAITING FOR SUMMER
by Sherelle Green, available November 2016
wherever Harlequin® Kimani Romance™
books and ebooks are sold.